Read more in the Hill School Girls series

Alone
Secrets
Strangers

Read more for middle readers from Duckbill

Ninja Nani and the Bumbling Burglars by Lavanya Karthik
Ninja Nani and the Mad Mummy Mix-up by Lavanya Karthik
Ninja Nani and the Zapped Zombie Kids by Lavanya Karthik
Against All Odds by Ramendra Kumar
The Case of the Candy Bandit by Archit Taneja
The Case of the Careless Aliens by Archit Taneja
Oops the Mighty Gurgle by RamG Vallath
The Deadly Royal Recipe by Ranjit Lal
Vanamala and the Cephalopod by Shalini Srinivasan
Flat-track Bullies by Balaji Venkataramanan
Ravana Refuses to Die by Rustom Dadachanji
Dhanak by Anushka Ravishankar and Nagesh Kukunoor
Simply Nanju by Zainab Sulaiman
Hot Chocolate is Thicker than Blood by Rupa Gulab
The Sherlock Holmes Connection by Martin Widmark, Anushka Ravishankar, Katarina Genar and Bikram Ghosh
Tiger Boy by Mitali Perkins
The Magicians of Madh by Aditi Krishnakumar
Pops! by Balaji Venkataramanan
Karma Fights a Monster by Evan Purcell
Karma Meets a Zombie by Evan Purcell
Ninja Nani and the Mad Mummy Mix-up by Lavanya Karthik
Neha and the Nose by Ruchika Chanana
The Piano: Story of a Friendship by Nandita Basu

THE HILL SCHOOL GIRLS

Trouble

A. COVEN

duckbill

An imprint of Penguin Random House

DUCKBILL BOOKS

USA | Canada | UK | Ireland | Australia
New Zealand | India | South Africa | China | Singapore

Duckbill Books is part of the Penguin Random House group of companies
whose addresses can be found at global.penguinrandomhouse.com

Published by Penguin Random House India Pvt. Ltd
4th Floor, Capital Tower 1, MG Road,
Gurugram 122 002, Haryana, India

Penguin Random House India

First published by Duckbill Books 2018

This edition published in Duckbill Books by Penguin Random House India 2020

10 9 8 7 6 5 4 3 2

ISBN 9789387103085

Typeset by PrePSol Enterprises Pvt. Ltd.

Printed at Repro India Limited

www.penguin.co.in

FSC www.fsc.org MIX Paper from responsible sources FSC® C047271

This is a legitimate digitally printed version of the book and therefore might not have certain extra finishing on the cover.

1

'So, already missing your new boyfriend?' Shernaz asked, as we drove to the station where she was going to put me on the train for Lailapaani.

My sister Shernaz and I had just got back after spending two weeks in Deolali cantonment at our uncle's place. I played basketball every day with my cousins Jamshed and Cyrus and their neighbour, Girish, who is really good at the game. He's the captain of his school team.

Girish would make a great basketball coach—I learnt so much from him! He corrected my stance and he taught me some cool ways to dribble around aggressive defenders. I've got pretty good at baskets, even. I once managed to put in three airballs in a row from the free-throw line!

Of course, Shernaz promptly started teasing me about Girish. 'He's quite hot, Maaz, for a teenaged boy. You can admit you have a crush on him,' she said.

'As if. Just because he's my Facebook friend, doesn't mean that we're romantically involved. You have a one-track mind these days and we all know why,' I shot back, pleased when she blushed. It's she who's all starry-eyed about that Lt Cherian, who came every single day to see her. It was beginning to get pretty pukey, the way they made sheep's eyes at each other.

My uncle laughed and called it a holiday romance, but I think it's more than that.

Mamma and Pappa were at the station to receive me. They were happy to see me, but I got the feeling that they were a bit worried. I wonder if Rusi Uncle said something to them about Lt C. I hope not.

I took a deep breath when I stepped out of the station. Deolali was lovely and all, but it was good to be back in Lailapaani.

I had one day before school reopened for the winter term. It was getting cold and the ground was covered with fallen leaves. Shernaz has always hated this time of the year in Lailapaani, but there's something about the air, with that shimmery winter light and that typical winter smell which makes me feel ridiculously happy.

'Mahruuukhhh!' screamed Maitreyi and Ayesha, waving madly from the back of the assembly hall as I entered.

Of course, they promptly got asked to move up to the front as punishment, by—who else—Indu Miss. So we ended up sitting right in front, again. To the irritation of Ayesha and Maitreyi, Elizabeth and I had somehow started sitting in the front row for the first-day assemblies. I don't know how it happened. I guess it's because ever since Hill School became Holistic, the first day of school has been very entertaining.

Elizabeth grinned wickedly as she came in and sat with us.

'Look who's sitting on the front bench these days!'

'Oh shaddup,' said Ayesha, with a mock scowl. Then she grinned. 'It's cool to be back! Can't wait to tell you guys about my vacation.'

'I wonder what surprise Palak Nanda is going to unleash on us this term,' said Elizabeth, looking around nervously, as if Palak Nanda was going to leap out from under the chairs yelling 'SURPRISE!'

We all looked at Maitreyi. As daughter of a teacher, she was expected to keep us informed. But she shrugged. 'Haven't heard a thing,' she said. 'I just got back today.'

'Guess where she was,' said Ayesha, waggling her eyebrows. She was Maitreyi's roommate, so she got all the news first.

'Nooo! You spent the *entire* vacation with your dad?' I couldn't believe it, after all the drama that had happened over her long-lost family last term.

Maitreyi looked sheepish, but before we could ask her anything else, a murmur went around the room. Palak Nanda had arrived to make the beginning-of-the-year announcements.

'So lovely to see you all looking so *fresh*, after your holidays. This term we have a really *lovely* set of activities planned for you. Last term Class VIII did a *stellar* job of setting up the school for the flood-affected children in Panipur, and this term, some of the other classes will have the wonderful opportunity to go and see how *well* the school is getting along.'

She went on to talk about nature trips, tree planting and other stuff that we would do during the term.

'But now comes the *exciting* part!' she exclaimed.

I didn't hold my breath. Palak Nanda's idea of exciting was probably watching a caterpillar hibernate or some such thing.

'At the end of the year, instead of a school play, we're going to have a unique project: it's going to be called the Holistic Showcase. The idea is to show your parents that you are not here *only* to study. Each class will have to come up with some aspect of your holistic development and *showcase* it to show how Hill School is about developing *all* your faculties.'

Oh my god. This was flaky even by Palak Nanda standards. I sighed, thinking this was going to be a really painful term.

I'd been a little worried when the school changed its name from Hill School Girls' School to Hill School for Holistic Learning. Holistic cow, I thought! I mean, what kind of name is that for a school?

At first, it was really weird. We had to do insane stuff like talk to trees. Really. But it had been getting better. We've been doing things that you would never get to do in any other school. Last term, we actually helped to set up a new school for kids who'd been affected by the floods in Panipur, which is in the upper mountains. Pretty radical. And we've had seminars about strange things, but they're also fun and kind of help us see things from a different point of view.

There are no exams any more, though we have to do project after project, which can get quite annoying, but it can also be exciting. One project ended up in Elizabeth, Ayesha,

Maitreyi and me breaking and entering into the home of an old woman, Ms Sultania, who's the granddaughter of the founder of our school. But she's our best friend now, so all's well.

Of course we've also had wacko things like dance-yoga and a hide-and-seek tournament for sports day (which, in case you hadn't guessed, was a complete disaster), but ah well, some things work and some things don't.

I was just getting used to it all, and thinking it wasn't so bad, and now this! A Holistic Showcase? Seriously?

Suddenly, Ayesha nudged me, and I snapped out of my irritated reverie. I looked towards the stage.

' ... represented India at the Olympics. We're really, *really* lucky to have her with us for one term,' Palak Nanda was saying.

I couldn't believe I had missed hearing this. 'What game? What game?' I hissed.

'Guess,' said Elizabeth dryly, nodding at the stage.

'Let me introduce Abha Gokhale!' said Palak Nanda, who suddenly looked like a dwarf. Because on the stage was the tallest woman I'd ever seen.

'A basketball coach,' I breathed, instantly forgiving Palak Nanda everything.

'Someone get Mahrukh some smelling salts,' whispered Maitreyi, chuckling. She started reading some old historical romance books last term and has since started saying these strange things, so I ignored her and concentrated on what Abha Gokhale was saying.

'I'm very happy to be here. I must say I was a bit reluctant at first, but Palak Ma'am spoke so passionately about the school and her vision for it that I feel really privileged to be here, to do my bit, even if it's only for one term. I'm not here only to teach you basketball. I would like to make all of you fall in love with all sports.'

'Mahrukh has already fallen in luurve,' sang Ayesha. She can be very annoying. But I ignored her too.

Basketball with an Olympic player! This was going to be a great term, after all!

During the break, I suggested we go to the canteen.

'I'm not hungry,' said Elizabeth, grumpily. We'd just been told by Eileen Miss that our grades this term would depend as much on participation and enthusiasm as on the actual content of our end-of-term projects. Ms Academix was miffed, of course. She hated any method of grading that was out of her control.

'I'm hungry,' declared Ayesha and Maitreyi, almost in chorus. So we headed to the canteen with Elizabeth trailing behind us, looking like the world had come to an end.

There was the usual rubbish in the canteen. We bought a couple of oily pakodas and went off to sit on our bench. Okay, not exactly our bench—it was the bench near the basketball court, where we usually had all our meetings and fights.

But when we got there, there were two girls sitting there, already. New girls, clearly. One of them had a ridiculously long fringe that almost covered her eyes. They looked miserable and scared. They must have been in Class V or VI, I guessed.

We went up to them and politely asked them if they could go sit somewhere else.

'But why?' asked the one without the fringe. She looked genuinely bewildered and I felt it was a fair question. I was about to explain, when Elizabeth butted in.

'Listen, new girl. If we say go, you go. That's it. NQA. No Questions Asked. Understood?'

Not exactly polite, I agree, but it was Elizabeth. As aggression goes, it would be about two on a one-to-ten scale, I'd have said. But the girls began to bawl! You'd think Elizabeth had launched a brutal attack on them. In fact, she looked more taken aback than the rest of us.

'Hey!' she said. 'Relax, it's okay. It's just that this is *our* usual place to hang out, so—'

'I knew it!' screamed the girl with the fringe. 'I told my mom that we would get ragged and bullied, but she didn't listen. We're just two of us and you're so many of you. You-you-you g-giant bullies!' And she began to howl even louder.

The four of us looked at each other, and we just couldn't help it. We started laughing. It must have been the 'giant' or maybe it was their expressions. It was also Elizabeth's totally wimpy attempt at being tough. I mean, where on earth did she dream up 'NQA'?? Or maybe it was just so good to be back together at Hill School again. Anyway, we went a bit hysterical.

The two howling girls got even more terrified and fled. Gasping and wheezing, we collapsed onto our bench.

Suddenly, a shadow loomed over us. It was Abha Gokhale.

'Shame on you,' she said.

I stood up, my laughter dying an abrupt death. Elizabeth got up stammering, 'G-g-good afternoon, Miss.' Ayesha was still half prone on the bench. Maitreyi tried to get up, gave a loud hiccup and subsided, giggling silently. She set Ayesha off again.

It wasn't very respectful, but I didn't at first understand why Abha Miss was looking so thunderous. Giggling foolishly wasn't such a big crime.

'I saw those poor girls crying,' she said, then, and the penny dropped. She thought we'd been bullying those two silly things! 'I have half a mind to report you.'

'Miss, no Miss, we didn't do anything Miss!' squeaked Elizabeth, terrified.

Abha Miss narrowed her eyes. 'Don't make it worse by lying, please. I will let you go this time, but let me not catch you doing anything like this again.' She looked at each of us in turn, as if searing our faces into her memory, then turned on her heel and strode away.

'Oh dear,' said Elizabeth helplessly.

I was dumbstruck. This was not how I had imagined meeting Abha Gokhale for the first time. She would hate me forever. She probably wouldn't allow me to train with her. I would have to give up basketball.

My life was ruined. And it was just the first day of term.

2

Since it was the first day and all, the hostelites were allowed to wander out in the evening. Usually, they were only allowed out on weekends.

So Maitreyi and Ayesha came with me to Empire Stores. Elizabeth had to go home, but she said she would join us later.

We had put a couple of little tables with chairs in a corner of the shop, and now people could have their bakery items and tea, coffee and cold drinks in the shop itself.

My parents had done this in the break while I was away. They felt we were losing customers to coffee shops, just because they had place to sit, though their baked goodies didn't hold a candle to ours. Our muffins, breads and cakes were famous in Lailapaani, and the locals would never buy their breads and muffins from anywhere else, but tourists weren't as picky. They just wanted to rest and have coffee and eat something somewhat edible.

'This is perfect!' Maitreyi said, her voice muffled by blueberry muffin. 'I wonder why those guys aren't here yet.'

'Those guys' were Maitreyi's recently-discovered brother, Oroon, and his friend Vir. Oroon was in Baldwin and we'd all got to know him because of the project last term, which we did with the Baldwin Boys' School. He was nothing like Maitreyi—they kind of resembled each other in looks, but they were completely different in temperament.

There was a sudden commotion at the front and we heard someone squealing with laughter. Oroon and Vir came in, laughing. Sheba, who had joined school last year, was with them. She was laughing too. Elizabeth trailed after them. She wasn't laughing. But then, she doesn't laugh a lot.

Ayesha waggled her eyebrows at Maitreyi and me. I knew what was in her mind. Last term, Sheba's so-called friend (she turned out not to be her friend at all, but that's another story), Ela, used to tease her about Oroon. I think it was just malice. I frowned at Ayesha and shook my head.

'What's funny?' Maitreyi asked her brother.

'Elizabeth nearly fell off her bike,' he grinned. No wonder Elizabeth wasn't laughing, then.

'I don't see why that's funny,' she grumbled, as she sat down with us. 'They jumped at me from nowhere, so it was not even my fault.'

We had to put all the tables together.

'If Mahrukh's friends hog all the chairs and tables, where will the other customers go, hunh?' Mamma said. But she was smiling, so everyone knew she was joking.

'We're customers too, Aunty!' said Ayesha, cheekily. 'Come on, people, give me your orders, I'll go and get them at the counter. Give me money also, okay, in case you're imagining this is my treat!'

While all this was going on, I noticed that Vir had grown really tall in the holidays. 'Vir, you've grown, like, several feet!' said Maitreyi, echoing my thought.

'How tall are you now?' I asked, enviously. I would kill to be so tall.

'Five eleven,' said Vir, looking a little bashful.

'You should play basketball!' said Elizabeth.

'He does,' Oroon replied. 'So do I.'

'You?' asked Sheba. 'But you're ...' she trailed off.

'Yeah yeah, I know. I may be small, but I'm sneaky!'

We all laughed. I liked Oroon. He was funny. And I was thrilled to know that they both played basketball. We were soon discussing the game. Oroon loved playing basketball, and knew a lot about famous American basketball players. When Ayesha and I told them we had an Olympic-level coach, their eyes nearly popped out of their heads!

'We have a new coach too,' said Vir. 'He's an ex-student. He's really cool.'

'Yeah, he was studying in Canada, and now he's back, coaching us,' said Oroon. 'His name is Anil ... something with H. Really long. Something-ani.'

'Not Anil Hiranandani!' I exclaimed. He used to be the local heartthrob. He was a couple of years senior to Shernaz, and I remember her friends constantly going gaga over him. He was supposed to be handsome and cool and a really good sportsman. Shernaz had never liked him, somehow. 'He got a sports scholarship in Ontario and went off soon after school. He couldn't have finished college, though.' I counted the years. 'Nope. No way he could have finished.'

This was interesting. I decided to tell Shernaz about it when she called later in the evening. Why would Hiro, as he was widely known back in the day, be here, teaching a bunch of kids basketball? He was supposedly quite a good student, as well as being a top-class jock.

Meanwhile, the talk at the table had moved on to what everyone had done in the vacations. Maitreyi and Oroon had spent the summer with their father. Maitreyi hadn't even met her father until the end of last term and I wondered what that must have been like. But as the two of them chattered away about the films they'd seen and some picnic or the other where they swam in a river and nearly drowned, I realised that it was all good. I suddenly wondered if Indu Miss had been lonely. She was used to having Maitreyi with her all the time. But it didn't seem like something I could ask.

It was strange to see everyone sitting here. I'm sure it seemed perfectly normal to all of them, but I could never see this place as a coffee shop. I couldn't even see it as a shop, actually. To me, Empire Stores was home.

'Oy!' yelled Ayesha. 'Stop dreaming! Let's tell them about our encounter with Miss Olympics today.'

Ugh. I wish she hadn't reminded me.

3

The next day, we had games. I'd been so looking forward to basketball this term, but now I dreaded it. I wondered for a moment if I should pretend to be ill. But in the end, I decided against it. There would be too many explanations.

We gathered on the sports field. Abha Miss looked at all of us and I'm pretty sure she scowled when she looked at Maitreyi, Ayesha, Elizabeth and me standing together. Shinie Miss, who used to teach us basketball, was now going to take all the other games, so that Abha Miss could concentrate on the basketball and athletic teams. I looked at her to see if she was upset, but she was gazing at Abha Miss with open admiration.

We were to divide ourselves up depending on which game we wanted to play. I chickened out at the last moment and chose kho-kho because Maitreyi and Elizabeth had chosen it. Maitreyi was incredibly good at it. Elizabeth hated all games, but she felt that at least kho-kho was something she hadn't tried. If she didn't choose some game, she would be made to run around the field every day with all the other girls who had opted out of team games. She hated that even more than she hated games.

‘What’s wrong with you?’ Ayesha whisper-shouted at me, grabbing my arm when I started going off with the kho-kho lot.

‘She hates us already. And anyway, kho-kho is fun.’

‘She doesn’t even know us. And don’t be an idiot. I won’t say kho-kho is lame, exactly, but come on! Basketball? Kho-kho?’ She did that weighing thing with both her hands, which she knows irritates me. But today I just shook my head and walked away.

I could feel Suchi, Tarini and the other girls I usually played basketball with staring at me. I guess they were really surprised. So was Shinie Miss.

‘What you’re doing here, Mahrukh? Not playing basketball?’

‘No Miss, I want to try kho-kho this year.’

‘You’re mad or what? Where you’ll get the chance to train with somebody like Abha Gokhale every day? Go, go, I don’t want you here.’

I was in such a fix. What could I say? And just then, Ayesha came bounding along.

‘Miss, can I take Mahrukh? We want her in the basketball team.’ She practically dragged me off.

I later found out that Abha Miss asked the girls about last year’s teams and games, and at some point everyone yelled out my name.

‘Who is Mahrukh?’ Abha Miss asked, looking around with a smile.

‘She’s gone off to play kho-kho, Miss!’ said Tarini.

Before Abha Miss could say anything to that, Ayesha volunteered to fetch me, and everyone cheered and all that. I really didn't know they wanted me so badly on the team! I'm just an okay player, so it's actually quite sweet.

I was still very, very nervous. So the team liked me, but what about Abha Miss?

She looked at me as we walked towards the basketball court, and raised her eyebrows, clearly surprised that a girl who was part of a gang of bullies could have so much support.

'You're overthinking this!' Ayesha hissed. 'I bet she doesn't even remember us. We all probably look like a big blob of schoolgirlness to her.'

Wrong.

'I would like all of you to work together as a group. I want you to know that I will not stand for bullying or one-upmanship in my team,' was one of the first things Abha Miss told us.

That was clearly meant for Ayesha and me. I could feel my ears going red. The other girls looked at Suchi. She was known for hogging the ball, refusing to pass and even pushing and hitting people. She'd been thrown out of the team once already but then Palak Nanda came and the old sports teacher, Arora Miss, left, so Suchi was back. But Abha Miss didn't know all that.

We were made to stand in a line and shoot baskets. Three turns each. I was tense. I had been shooting baskets all through the vacation, but this was different. I could feel Miss looking at me suspiciously. I felt like I had BULLY written on my forehead, which was ridiculous because I hadn't ever bullied anyone in my life.

My palms were sweaty when Ayesha threw me the ball. I caught it and took a shot at once, without waiting to gauge the distance or position myself properly. The ball slipped out of my damp palms at an odd angle and went off far to the left of the basket and so low that it almost hit Monica on her head.

I wished I could disappear in a puff of smoke.

'Come on, Mahrukh, you can do this!' Ayesha yelled, throwing me the ball once again.

I took a deep breath. This was getting ridiculous. I had done nothing wrong, why was I feeling guilty? And so what if Abha Miss thought I was horrible? And so what if she was an Olympic player? So what? I wiped my hands on my skirt, weighed the ball in my hands, crouched and took a shot, the way Girish had taught me.

It went in without even hitting the board. I grunted, feeling rather pleased, while the girls all clapped. I didn't dare look at Miss. Someone threw me the ball again and I took aim again. Another clean basket. All that work in the summer had clearly paid off.

There was such a buzzing in my ears that I didn't hear anything, though I could see some of the others yelling things at me. I went and stood next to Ayesha. She nudged me hard. She has such sharp elbows!

'What?' I mumbled. I still didn't dare to look towards Miss.

'Nothing,' grinned Ayesha. 'That was cool!'

I finally looked up and grinned back at her. As we did a high-five, I caught a glimpse of Abha Miss from the corner of my eye. She was looking at us, and she was not smiling.

My heart dropped to my toes, but I decided I was not going to let it bother me. I was going to focus on my game. That's all that mattered.

To my delight, we had games every day this term. I think good old Palak Nanda was trying to maximise the advantage of having Abha Miss with us.

So the basketball team met every day. But we weren't playing much basketball, I have to say.

We spent half the period doing warm-ups. While we did that, Abha Miss worked with the track and field athletes.

Then she came back and made us do all sorts of basic drills. We spent two days just doing ball-handing drills—finger grabs, slapping and tipping the ball from hand to hand, dropping and catching ... it was repetitive, but so useful! I realised most of us were holding the ball wrong, in the first place.

Some of the girls soon began to get fed up.

'We want to play, Miss!' whined Suchi when we'd been doing drills for four days straight.

'You're not ready to play,' Abha Miss told her. 'I said finger grab! You're touching the ball with your palm again. Mahrukh, come here and show everyone the figure-eight. Girls, try and follow her.'

I was thrilled, but of course I didn't show it. The figure-eight is a cool drill. You move the ball between your legs in a figure-of-eight, passing it from hand to hand. You're supposed to look up as you do it, and not drop the ball, obviously.

It's harder than it looks and it was a while before everyone got it. Some of them couldn't manage it at all.

'She likes you!' Ayesha said grinning wickedly. We were trudging back slowly to class—figure-eights were hell on the back and knees.

I shrugged. I think Abha Miss just appreciated hard work, and I was really working hard. When she looked at me, I could still see the disapproval in her eyes. But I was learning basketball the way it should be learned. I was happy with that.

4

There was chaos and commotion in the class.

Eileen Miss had just told us that we had until the end of the day to come up with an idea for the Holistic Showcase at the end of the year.

Everyone started talking at the same time, and for a few minutes, no one could hear anyone else speak. I don't think anyone quite understood what a Holistic Showcase meant—not even Miss.

'Miss, what exactly do we have to do?' Ayesha asked, putting her on the spot.

'Er ... umm, showcase your, you know, *holistic* development, as opposed to just your, er, academic progress.'

'Yes, but what does that mean?' asked Ayesha.

'Games, Miss! Let's have a friendly match between us, to showcase our development in sports,' Suchi suggested.

'Yes, or even a race!' said Prerna.

'Mm, that's not a bad idea ... but ...'

'Miss, let's collect as many insects as we can find and classify them and do an exhibition,' I called out. 'That's pretty holistic, Miss! It's biology, environment and ...'

'And gross!' Ayesha said.

'Miss, if all the classes do something extracurricular, then maybe we can showcase our academics, no, Miss? After all, holistic *includes* academics.' That was Elizabeth, of course.

Finally, it was Maitreyi who came up with a neat solution. 'Miss, the project our class did with building the school in Panipur last year was totally holistic. Why don't we do an exhibition of that? We have photos, and we can get people to write up their experiences.'

'I know!' said Ayesha, 'We can make a website about it! That'll be even more holistic, because it'll show we did all that *and* we know how to work with technology.'

Miss looked so relieved I thought she was going to cry. She quickly put Maitreyi and Ayesha in charge.

'Maitreyi,' said Ayesha in the break, chomping on a lacy papad-like thing called achappam that Elizabeth had brought from home, 'you're a genius.'

'Comes from going to alternative schools all my life. I know exactly what works. This is positively dull compared to some of the things I've had to do. In my last school, we had to do a performance combining painting and music and dance. So when someone played a tune, the kids who were assigned to painting had to "paint the tune" and the dancers had to dance. Thank god I was in the dance team. The poor painters looked completely confused. They just did whatever they felt like and then they had a fight in the middle of the show and finally they all left the stage crying. What do you expect—we were in Class V, we had no clue what was going on!'

'Yikes!' I said. 'And I thought the Holistic Showcase was weird!'

'We've already got all the library stuff on computer, so that's easy to do. We'll just need pictures of the library,' said Elizabeth.

Maitreyi and Elizabeth had opted for the library group when we were helping with the school last year. They were called the Bookies. Ayesha had been part of the Geeks, in charge of systems and all the computer stuff.

'And the garden!' I said. I was really proud of how we'd set up the garden in the school. We'd done our research and taken a lot of care to see that the plants we chose would not harm the ecology of the hills. The plants must have grown, and I was quite eager to see how the garden looked now.

'We can ask Sara to take pictures for us,' said Ayesha.

'You ask her, Ayesha, she'll do annnnnything for you!' teased Maitreyi. Sara hero-worshipped Ayesha. It embarrassed her, and so, obviously, we never missed a chance to tease her about it.

At games, Abha Miss made an electrifying announcement—we were going to play our first match next week! We were going to play against Modern School, which was one of the most fancy schools in Lailapaani.

All thought of gardens and photographs flew out of my head. We had done so little actual playing that none of us had expected this.

'But Miss!' wailed Suchi. 'We haven't actually played any basketball.'

'So think of this as a practice game,' said Abha Miss. 'You can try out all the skills we've been practising. In fact, we'll have a go today. We'll have a match.'

This was so exciting! We quickly divided ourselves up into two teams.

'Right,' said Miss. 'Just one thing. I don't want to focus only on scoring baskets. I will be watching you carefully to see if you're doing good dribbles, keeping all the ball-holding tips in mind and making the right passing decisions.' We groaned. 'I also want to see you use some of the defence and offence strategies that we have been working on. Now go. Huddle first, plan your tactics and let me know when you're ready.'

'We need to choose a captain,' said Ayesha, who was on the same team as me. 'I vote for Mahrukh.' To my dismay, everyone agreed instantly. I didn't want to be captain! It was too much pressure. I just wanted to relax and enjoy the first proper game I'd played in weeks.

Once we'd decided positions, we made some tactical decisions. Most importantly, we decided to keep an eye on Suchi. I'm not a great fan of man-to-man defence, but we needed to do that with Suchi, so Ayesha was given the job.

'Be careful, though,' I warned Ayesha. 'She throws a mean punch!'

We really enjoyed the game. We fumbled with the ball, forgot some basic things that Abha Miss had been trying to drill into us and missed more baskets than we scored, but it was just so exhilarating to be on the court playing an actual game!

In the end, Suchi's team (she had made herself captain)

scored two points more than us. But we didn't really care. She'd been playing rough, as usual, and we knew she was going to get it from Miss.

Abha Miss called us together at the end. 'Pathetic!' she said. 'I knew you'd forget some of the things you've learnt, but this is really shocking, after so many weeks of practice.'

All the excitement of the game drained out in a big whoosh, and I felt completely deflated. Pathetic. Abha Miss thought we were pathetic.

'We won, Miss!' Suchi shouted.

'Your team played a completely unacceptable game! What was that? I went easy on fouls, otherwise more than half your baskets would have been disqualified. I don't call that winning.' Suchi looked sulky. 'The other team,' she looked at us, 'was slow and took too long to decide the play, but you were at least making an attempt to apply what you've been learning in the last few weeks. So, well done.'

'Yay,' I muttered. The rest of the team didn't look exactly ecstatic either.

'Okay, now stop looking so gloomy. We have almost a week before the match. And it's only a friendly match, so don't so get stressed about it. We'll practice some plays. Some of you are shaping up really well. I saw some nice moves today and we'll work on them. Don't worry, we'll be ready for those girls when they come! Now, we need to choose a captain.'

Ayesha promptly put up my hand. I pulled it down. 'No!' I said.

Suchi put up her hand.

Abha Miss was quiet for a minute. Then, 'Ayesha, Tarini and Mahrukh, come here. The rest of you can disperse.'

'Miss,' I said quickly, before my feet could get cold, 'I really don't want to be captain. Half the time today I was focussed on what the others were doing and I felt it affected my game.'

'Yes, I saw that. But you're thinking strategy, so I need you to be involved. Tarini, you will be captain and Ayesha will be vice-captain, but I want all three of you to help me come up with a game plan. Mahrukh will be shooting guard. You know what that means?'

We shook our heads, but I had an idea what it was, and it was giving me a strange feeling in my stomach, because it meant Abha Miss actually thought I was a good player.

'You will set up the offensive plays, basically. And you're also one of the best long-distance shots. So you'll be pivotal to the team.'

'Whoa! Don't pass out, now!' said Ayesha, nudging me with her killer elbow.

Abha Miss laughed. We discussed a few more things and then I went home with Elizabeth and Rakshita.

When I neared Empire Stores, I saw a tall, well-dressed man leaving the shop. He had a scowl on his face. He got into a Mercedes that was parked outside and drove away. He wasn't one of our regular customers. I ran in, bursting with my news, but stopped short at the door, with shock.

My mother and father were arguing. They *never* argue. Shernaz and I always giggled at them for calling each other 'darling' and holding hands while watching TV. They never even raised their voices at one another. Or at us. And now they were shouting! I felt my palms get cold instantly. It was terrifying—it was like seeing the sun rise from the west or watching water flow upwards.

'No!' Mamma was yelling. 'No! We won't! No!'

'You're being unrealistic, Shireen,' said Pappa and his voice was loud too, though it quivered a bit, which was even more frightening. 'Times have changed. We have to accept! We knew this was coming. How long has it been since we made a profit on this place? How long can we go on like this? We'll have to sell.'

Sell? Sell what? Sell our shop? Empire Stores was so much part of my life that I'd never really bothered to think about it. It was there, like the earth and the sky and the hills. It was home, more than our house was. Shernaz and I grew up behind the counters of the shop.

When we were smaller and Mamma and Pappa were working, we'd spread out a rug on the floor and eat, read, play games and pretty much live there. Our house was right next door, but it was much more exciting to be in the shop, watching the people who came and went and smelling the fresh bread and muffins that were baking in the bakery at the back.

Now it seemed like my sky was going to fall on my head. I'd seen the signs and ignored them.

When my great-grandfather started the shop, it used to be the only one in town and had groceries, baked goods, cloth, stationery, cosmetics and all sorts of odd things under one roof. Our sign used to say: 'Empire Stores. We Keep Everything.'

Then the fancy chain stores began to open up and people began to buy things online, so no one came to us for odds and ends any more. We stopped keeping cloth, except material for school uniforms and some handmade lace that came from Mumbai. Supermarkets had come up all over town, so Pappa and Mamma had reduced groceries. We still kept the stuff that our regular customers wanted, and local specialties like jams and preserves and cheeses, but there wasn't so much variety any more. The Hill School and Baldwin students came to us for their stationery. We also kept goodies for the schoolchildren, because we were the closest to both the schools. Our muffins were still famous.

Our sign now said simply: 'Empire Stores & Bakery'.

I should have paid more attention. I should have realised that Mamma and Pappa were finding it difficult to keep the shop going. When I got back from my vacation, I'd noticed they were looking ragged, but I never really asked why.

'We'll come up with something. We can't give in to this kind of arm-twisting. That rogue! That shark!' Mamma was still shouting.

'He *is* a rogue and a shark, but there's the mortgage,' Pappa said.

'What's a mortgage?' I asked. My voice, to my embarrassment, was kind of wobbly and hoarse.

'Oh, dikra!' Mamma said. 'When did you come? I'm so sorry you had to walk in to this! It's my fault for losing my cool.' She came and gave me a big hug.

I swallowed sudden tears and asked again, 'Tell me about the mortgage?'

Mamma and Pappa looked at one another. They held hands. My world righted itself just a little bit.

'Come,' Pappa said. We closed the shop—something we never do during shop hours—and went home.

5

We had a family conference that evening. Mamma called Shernaz and put her on the speaker.

Then Pappa told us what had been happening under our very noses, which Shernaz and I, living in our own world of school, college, friends and games, had completely missed.

A few years ago, Pappa and Mamma had had to take a loan from the bank—they didn't say, but we knew why. None of us could forget those months of uncertainty when Mamma was ill and we didn't know if she would survive. She had had cervical cancer and she had been in and out of the hospital for months. Pappa aged ten years in those fourteen months. But Mamma recovered and we'd all grown used to skirting around the subject of her illness, trying to pretend it had never happened.

At that time, the shop and the house had been mortgaged to the bank against the loan. Which meant that the bank kind of owned our shop and our house now. As long as the interest for the loan was paid regularly, it was fine. But in the past six months or so, because the shop was doing so badly, we hadn't been able to pay the interest.

And now the bank was threatening to auction off the property, if we didn't pay up. The bank manager was a friend of my parents, so he had warned them that this was going to happen. He was trying to stave it off as long as possible, but things had come to a head. If Pappa didn't pay up within two months, we might lose our shop and our house!

'Two months! Where are we going to get so much money in two months?' I asked.

'Did you ask Darius Uncle?' Shernaz asked.

'No, dikri, we couldn't ask him,' said Pappa. 'He wants to send Jamshed to college in America, and he'll need a lot of money for that. It's not easy on an army salary, baba. If we ask him, he won't be able to say no.'

Typical Pappa. Think of everyone else's problems first.

'Why didn't you tell me?' Shernaz wailed. 'I could have gone to college in Lailapaani. Hostel is so expensive! I'm going to transfer.'

'Don't you dare,' said Mamma. 'We'll work this out.'

'Then I'll get a job,' said Shernaz.

'Shernaz ...' Mamma began, when I butted in.

'But Mamma,' I asked, 'what has all this got to do with that man I saw?'

That man, it turned out, was Rajmohan Sisodia, who had built most of the new buildings in Lailapaani. He was a contractor. I knew his name because of the ugly complex of multi-storied flats which was called Sisodia Park View. It was a dirty pink to begin with and once it had got through a few monsoons, it had turned streaky and even dirtier.

Shernaz and I hated it, because before it was built we could see right across the valley from the window of our room. And now we could only see balconies with people's clothes hanging from them. Because of his Park View, we had lost our view of the park.

'He came to–' Mamma swallowed and couldn't speak.

'He wants to buy us up. He's bought that old bungalow at the back that belonged to old Brigadier Gomes, and if he gets our land, it becomes a big property. He wants to build a mall.'

'NOOOOO!' Shernaz and I shouted together.

'And,' said Mamma, her voice rising in indignation, 'he says that if we don't sell it to him now, he'll make sure he buys it up cheap at the auction and kicks us out on the street.'

'Er ... he didn't exactly say–' Pappa began, but Mamma cut him off.

'He might as well have! What else did he mean by all those veiled threats, hunh? He started off being suave and friendly. I even made him a cup of coffee! But when we said no thank you, he showed his true colours. Very smooth he was, but finally, a threat is a threat, whether it's done with a snarl or with a smile.'

'Pappa!' I cried. 'Were you really thinking of selling Empire Stores to that horrible man?'

Pappa sighed. 'I don't want to, of course I don't. But we're really, really strapped for money, girls. If we don't sell, we have to come up with the interest quickly. I know it'll break all our hearts, but we can buy a small place somewhere with the money. It's not the end of the world.' He sounded exactly like it was the end of the world, so no one was convinced.

'But you know, Pappa,' said Shernaz, sounding thoughtful. 'If he's offering to buy it now, instead of waiting for the auction, it means he's in a hurry. Something's up.'

I didn't say anything, but I decided to talk to Shernaz later and go sleuthing a little bit. We needed to find out why this smooth operator was in such a hurry.

Meanwhile, there was the question of the money. How were we going to get so much so quickly?

The next day at school, I was still getting my head around it all.

'What's with the glum face, Mahrukh?' Maitreyi asked as soon as I entered the class.

'Nothing, just things,' I mumbled. I couldn't talk about it.

We had social studies with Indu Miss. She's quite scary, but I kind of like her. We were trying to wheedle a free period out of her, so that we could work on the showcase.

'Please, please, Miss! Ahmed Sir is free for a bit now, and we *have* to get started on the website. Why don't you come with us to the lab, Miss, then you can see that we're really going to work.'

Ayesha and I shot a grin at one another. We'd decided last term, for no good reason, that Indu Miss and Ahmed Sir were soft on each other. Knowing Indu Miss, I wouldn't be surprised if Ayesha's gambit backfired completely. But to my surprise, she said okay. She didn't come to the lab, though.

'You really must stop flogging that silly idea!' Elizabeth told us. Ayesha and I giggled.

'It's just fun to see Maitreyi's face when we say these things,' Ayesha said.

We spent the next two periods in the computer lab. Ayesha had given us all work to do, putting together stuff for the different pages that would go into the website. Sara had taken pictures for us when her class went to see the school at Panipur. The garden seemed to be doing really well; it was so good to see the plants grow and flower and fruit.

We uploaded the pictures in the folder that Ayesha had created. We then made a list of the seeds and saplings we had planted, with their biological names, their local names and a line about them. We also wrote a sort of summary about how we had gone about deciding what to plant in our garden—making sure we had seasonals as well as perennials, flowers as well as fruits, vegetables, herbs and ferns. As far as possible, we'd also stuck to indigenous varieties.

We were quite pleased with how our section of the website was shaping up.

In the break, we made our way to our bench, after the daily stop at the canteen. I don't know how Maitreyi and Ayesha could bear to eat that rubbish. We brought them snacks whenever we could but sometimes we didn't, and then they'd eat the slop from the canteen. They needed the variety, I guess, after the boring healthy food in the school mess. The canteen usually had only some biscuits, sev and other packaged snacks like that and oily pakodas and samosas.

'Ugh!' said Maitreyi. 'These samosas are chewy. Where are they getting these from?'

'Better than this,' Ayesha said, holding up a biscuit. 'So hard! I don't know why they're called nankhatai. They should call them nonteethai. Because once you eat it, you'll have no teeth left. I think I'll suggest that to Canteen Aunty.'

Ayesha began to hit the biscuit with a stone, so that she could break it into small pieces that would fit in her mouth.

'Eek. So unhygienic, Ayesha!' said Elizabeth.

'I bet this stone is cleaner than the biscuit. I bet this biscuit was mined from somewhere deep in the earth. It's a rare kind of rock. It couldn't have come from any bakery.'

A vague idea began to form in my head.

6

It was an eventful weekend, and that's putting it mildly.

On Friday, at basketball, Abha Miss had told us something that terrified and excited us. At the end of the year, Hill School was going to host a basketball tournament. All the schools in the district would be participating.

But first, we would need to repair the basketball court, and also construct a new one, otherwise the tournament would go on for like two years or something.

'But Miss, what will we do, then? Where will we practise?' wailed Monica.

'Give me some credit, Monica. I've figured that out,' said Abha Miss. She had very little patience with whiners. 'The new court will take a while, but the old court will be ready in a couple of days. So until then, alternative arrangements have been made. For our practice tomorrow, we're going to Baldwin.'

There was much gasping, giggling and tittering amongst the girls. Ayesha and I rolled our eyes at each other.

On Saturday morning, the team gathered at Hill School. Everyone was in a state of giddy excitement.

I was quite looking forward to seeing the Baldwin team, not just because Oroon and Vir would be there, but it would be interesting to see how the team was shaping up under the coaching of heartthrob Hiro.

When we got to Baldwin, we saw the team playing on one of the courts. They had three courts, but they were spread out over the grounds, so we weren't very close to them. We lined up at the edge of our court.

'Er girls, I'm standing here!' said Abha Miss, and all the heads whipped around. Miss was trying not to smile. 'We'll go take a look at their game later, but for now, let's concentrate on ours. You have a match coming up next week. It'll be useful to watch the Baldwin team, though, not just to check out if they have any interesting plays, but also because you might have to play them in the tournament.'

'What??' I don't know who shouted, but it was exactly my thought.

'Boys' team, Miss?'

'Yes, Palak Ma'am has decided that we will have mixed teams for the basketball tournament. So the co-ed schools will have both boys and girls on the same team. Baldwin, obviously, will field a team of boys.'

'But Miss, we'll lose, Miss. They're so big and they'll be rough,' said Suchi, whose style was totally cramped by Miss's strict no-pushing rules.

'That's why you have to polish your game, girls. You have to beat brawn with brain and agility. Come on, let's get started.'

An hour later, sweating and panting, we made our way to the other court, where the Baldwin team was still playing. I wondered if we were going to have to play the hulks who were sitting beside the court. The boys on the court looked a bit less daunting.

'You'll be playing the middle-level team,' Abha Miss said when we asked her. 'The big guys are the senior team, so they won't be part of the tournament.'

That was a relief.

We settled down around the court to watch. I looked at Anil Hiranandani, and I could see why he was such a heartthrob. He was tall and fair and good-looking in a classical sort of way. He was wearing dark glasses and he kept pushing his hair back when it flopped onto his forehead.

He came over to speak to Abha Miss, and he sounded really nice, too. Friendly and funny and very polished.

Abha Miss told him that we'd come to watch the boys play.

'Well, too bad you came so late, ma'am. We've just finished. Another time, maybe?'

'I guess. It'll be good for the girls to play the boys some time. Let's try and organise that?'

'If you like,' Hiro replied, but he didn't sound enthusiastic.

Ayesha and I waved to Oroon and Vir, who were on the court. They didn't wave back.

'That's weird. Think they didn't see us? But they're looking this way,' Ayesha said.

'You know what else is weird?' I whispered. 'They look like they're going to continue playing, so why's Hiro saying that they've finished?'

But the coach went back and said something to the boys, and they walked off the court. Oroon looked back once, but he turned away quickly. Something about the body language of the players struck me as strange, but I couldn't put my finger on it.

We headed back to the school, and then I walked home. Ayesha and Maitreyi were coming over in the evening and Elizabeth would come too. The four of us were going to meet Ms Sultania.

I got home to a huge surprise—Shernaz had come over for the weekend!

'Why did nobody tell me?' I cried.

'Because nobody knew,' Mamma said, giving Shernaz a stern look.

'But Mamma, how could I not come, when all this is happening here? We need to decide what to do. I'll be back on Monday morning, so I'm not even missing classes!'

'What is there to decide? We have to sell. It's just a question of when and how. Pappa has gone to talk to Mr Shenoy from the bank. He'll advise us correctly.'

I told Shernaz about our encounter with Anil Hiranandani. 'Why do you think he's doing this—coaching school kids, I mean? Didn't he go to Canada on a scholarship or something?'

'Hmm, I'll find out. I'm meeting some of the gang this evening. Someone might have heard something.'

We also speculated on why Mr S was in such a hurry to get us to sell. If the bank was anyway planning to do the auction in two months, wouldn't it be better for him to wait? Unless he was expecting someone else to bid much higher!

When Pappa came, we all pounced on him.

'Wait, wait, let me get my breath back, let me drink some water, let me find out why my daughter has turned up without notice,' he twinkled.

There must be good news, surely there must be, for him to be in such a cheerful mood? I kept my fingers crossed.

'So?' Mamma asked.

'It's not bad news, but it still leaves us with the big question of how to get the money,' Pappa said. 'Shenoy has managed to convince the loans department to give us more time, but we have to pay up two quarters' interest by the end of the month.'

'Is that a lot?' Shernaz asked anxiously.

'Not huge, but more than we've been making from the store of late,' Pappa said sadly. 'If we had a couple of big orders, we could tide over this. Then we'd have time to figure out the rest.'

'We'll think of something!' Shernaz said.

'What if we sell off some of the antique furniture in the house?' I asked.

'We can't sell anything from the house. Part of the mortgage,' Mamma said, sounding gloomy.

'Not even the new fryer?' I suggested.

Pappa snorted. 'Mahrukh, it's a small amount, but not that small. We have to think *outside the box*.' He'd clearly just heard this phrase from somewhere. Maybe from Mr Shenoy.

That's when the vague idea that had been forming in my head crystallised into a proper thought.

'We need to think in the box!' I said incoherently. The three of them looked at me in alarm. They clearly thought that all the tension had finally tipped the fine balance of my sanity. But then I explained my idea to them. Why not sell our muffins in the school canteen? They'd sell in huge numbers!

'We've approached the school before, but they've always said no.'

'No, Mamma, she's right!' Shernaz said. 'That was before Palak Nanda. The previous administrator used to get a cut from the canteen contractors. That's why she refused us. But it's not like that now. Now it's all in Palak Nanda's hands and she's very principled.'

'The canteen food is gross. Our fresh hot muffins will sell like ... well, like hot cakes,' I ended lamely.

The rest of the day passed in a blur. Phone calls, budgets, proposals ... The shop was open too, so we were all working—serving coffee, working at the cash counter, helping with the proposal. It felt good. I was so glad Shernaz had come and I think, in the end, Mamma and Pappa were, too.

When she came back from meeting her friends in the evening, I asked Shernaz if she had got any information about the Baldwin basketball coach. But she hadn't. Apparently, he'd been lying low and hadn't contacted any of his old friends.

'Not at all like him,' said Shernaz, and was about to tell me more, when her phone rang. From the way her ears went pink, I guessed it was Lt Cherian. From the way she spoke for, like, an hour, I knew it was.

On our way back from Ms Sultania's, I wondered whether to tell the others about all that had been happening, but before I could make up my mind, we heard a yell. Oroon and Vir were waving at us from across the road. There was another boy with them. I remembered seeing him on the basketball court.

They crossed over and we walked to Empire. The café was full, so we sat on the steps outside, eating cream rolls and drinking cold coffee.

'Why did you guys ignore us yesterday?' I asked.

Oroon and Vir looked at each other.

'And don't try to say you didn't see us because we saw you seeing us,' Ayesha added.

'Yes, we saw you see us see you,' grinned Oroon.

'Ha ha,' said Maitreyi. 'Who'd have thought my brother would turn out to be a stand-up comic. Not.'

'We're waiting,' I said.

The third boy, whose name was Nadeem, spoke up. He had a strong Brit accent. What was with these Baldwin boys? Oroon spoke like an American, anyway, and now this Nadeem sounded exactly like Daniel Radcliffe. Thank god for Vir's good old Punjabi accent, otherwise we'd all feel like we were in some alternate reality.

'It's really toxic out there,' Nadeem said. 'Anil encourages the bullies and they're getting out of hand. We're afraid to say or do anything.'

'But isn't he a good coach?'

'Well, yeah,' said Oroon, 'he is, kind of. He really knows his stuff, but he's quite rough, you know?'

'He encourages fouling and pushing, and he yells and throws the ball hard at anyone who he thinks is not doing what he wants them to,' Vir explained.

'Suchi would be right at home there,' said Elizabeth.

'Everyone's scared,' Nadeem said. 'We don't want to stop playing the game, so we carry on. Though honestly, even if we did want to stop, we'd be afraid to say!'

This was terrible. 'Does everyone feel this way?'

'No, I'll correct that. Not everyone. There are some guys who actually enjoy it. Mostly guys in the senior team. They get yelled at too, but they seem to thrive in that kind of angry environment.'

'They're the ones who're getting impossible. They would take every chance to get rough with us. That's why we didn't wave back. We didn't want to, you know ... attract attention to ourselves. Sorry!'

Before they left, the boys made us swear we wouldn't talk to anyone about this. I thought back to the morning and realised that what I had sensed in the Baldwin team as they walked away was fear.

7

The court wasn't ready on Monday, but Abha Miss decided we'd do field exercises and some passing drills instead. I was relieved. I really didn't feel like going to Baldwin and meeting the coach from hell.

By Tuesday, we were back to our court and practising like crazy. I was doing well with my shots—my training in the holidays had really come in useful! I suddenly remembered that I'd promised Girish I would keep in touch, but I'd completely forgotten to reply to his last message on FB.

In computer class that day, I finished off my assignment quickly so that I could log on to FB—Ahmed Sir allowed us to, as long as we took permission for a fixed amount of time.

I replied to Girish's message and told him about Abha Gokhale. I bet he'd be madly jealous! I didn't know what else to say. All we had in common was basketball. But he was nice and it was great to be able to talk (in a manner of speaking) to someone who was as obsessed about the game as I was.

In the break, I announced that I was treating everyone.

'Why?' asked Elizabeth, always suspicious. 'It's not your birthday for months. Has something happened?'

'No, Shernaz gave me some money before she left.'

The canteen was crowded, but I managed to go up and get four muffins.

'Muffins? In the canteen?' squealed Maitreyi, grabbing one. We went to our usual spot, sat down and bit into the muffins. At least, the others did. I was watching them.

'Mmmmmm ...' said Ayesha, mouth full and eyes closed.

Elizabeth was looking at her muffin as if it would bite her back. 'Wait a minute,' she frowned. 'I know this muffin.'

'Really? Were you properly introduced to it?' giggled Maitreyi.

But Elizabeth was looking a question at me. I nodded, grinning. Ayesha looked at the two of us.

'They're from your shop! No wonder they're so delish! Yippee! Does that mean we're going to get these muffins every day?'

'I hope so,' I said. And finally told them what had been going on.

Palak Nanda had agreed to have us supply muffins to the canteen. We'd started with only a few, but we were sure the orders would increase. We were to have a trial period of two weeks. If it went well, she'd agreed to give us an advance, which would help us pay off the immediate amount that Pappa had committed to. I told them all about the horrible Mr S and his threats.

'I've heard about this Sisodia guy! My father was talking about him the other day,' said Elizabeth. Her father was in the Forest Department. 'I wish I'd paid more attention to what he was saying. You know how he goes on about his trees, I just switch off sometimes.'

'Maybe he's a poacher!' saidMaitreyi.

Elizabeth gave her a look. 'Poaching what? Squirrels? There's no wildlife left in these forests any more. They've all migrated across the mountain to the Reserve. Only the monkeys are left and very few deer, and even those are dying from eating plastic.'

'True,' said Maitreyi, and shifted her attention back to her muffin.

'Don't worry,' said Ayesha, patting her stomach contentedly, 'these muffins are so good that the orders are going to hit the roof.'

It felt good to have told my friends about the trouble at Empire Stores. Suddenly, it didn't seem so scary any more. We'd manage.

The muffin business began to pick up, just as Ayesha had predicted. The canteen began to order puffs as well. We'd also put out word that we would do deliveries for parties and other large orders. In just a week, my parents had to hire new staff for the deliveries. Palak Nanda called to ask if we could cater muffins and puffs for the basketball match. That was going to be a whopping order! If things went on like this, we'd be out of the woods very soon.

We were all psyched up for the match. We'd been working really hard. The day scholars stayed back after school and all of us practised shooting baskets and passing and dribbling until Abha Miss had to actually force us to leave.

On the day of the match, I woke up early to help Mamma and Pappa pack up the muffins and puffs into boxes, ready to take to the school later on.

'That's enough! We'll do the rest,' Pappa tugged at my ponytail. 'I haven't seen you so bright-eyed and bushy-tailed in a long time.'

I giggled. I wish I'd had some premonition of what a nightmare this day was going to turn out to be. But I didn't, as I skipped off to play my first basketball match with Abha Gokhale as coach!

The team met on the court a couple of hours before the match. We were going to plan some plays and practise them for an hour, then rest for an hour before the match. Many of our friends had turned up early too. Abha Miss had said it was only a friendly match, but it was the first one we'd had in a while, and everyone was excited.

Though privately, we wondered how 'friendly' it would be. Palak Nanda looked at the whole world through a rosy prism, so she probably called the Modern School principal and said something like: 'Let's have a *friendly* match! Wouldn't it be nice if our students and your students could play as *friends* instead of *rivals*?'

Right. Like that was going to happen. The Modern School lot were snooty and uber-competitive. They'd always had a very good basketball team, and whenever we'd played with them, we'd lost badly. And they were really bad winners. They hooted and clucked and made up rude chants. We hadn't played against them since Palak Nanda took over, so she had no idea.

Before the match, Abha Miss called us all together.

'So team, all set?'

There was a muted scatter of 'Yes miss'es.

'What? Is that all the energy you can muster? I know you've been beaten by this team before, but you're not the same team now! You have some very strong players, you have excellent strategies in place, and you've worked your butts off.' She looked a bit embarrassed, so we realised she hadn't meant to say 'butts'. We giggled. 'You have!' Abha Miss grinned. 'Look, it's a game. No matter what you do, you could win, you could lose. But just go out there and do your stuff, and have fun doing it! Give it all you've got. Then win or lose is immaterial.'

'But Miss, we have to win! How can we win if we say it's okay to lose?' You had to admire Suchi's attitude sometimes!

'Play to win, girls, but don't be afraid to lose. Now go out there and get them!'

We ran out to the courts to loud applause and cheering. There was a huge crowd! We hadn't expected that at all. All the hostel girls had turned up, many day scholars had given up their precious Saturday to come and watch and there was a big contingent from Modern School as well.

The Modern School team was already at the court. They looked towards us, and someone said something. The rest of them snickered. I caught the word 'shorties'. The Modern School girls were, on an average, taller than us. I guess they had a minimum height for joining the team, whereas the Hill School philosophy was that anyone who wanted to play was allowed to be on the team.

Height is an advantage on the basketball court, but only if it comes with skill. If both teams were equally skilled, then their height was going to give them the edge.

When we huddled before the whistle, Monica said, 'Girls, they may have the height and history on their side, but this time we have a secret weapon! We have Abha Gokhale!'

'Let's do this for Abha Miss!' Ayesha said, and we all cheered. I was pleased to see that the Modern girls looked rattled. We'd never been so pumped up in our earlier skirmishes.

I wish I could say that we went out there and slayed them. We did nothing of the sort. We started slow, missed some fabulous chances and gave them some lollipop shots. By half-time, they were in the lead.

Abha Miss looked at our dejected faces. 'What is wrong with you girls?'

'Sorry, Miss,' I muttered.

'Sorry? What are you sorry for, Mahrukh? You're trailing by four points, four! That's all. Yes, you could have been leading now, but hey. This is your first real match as a team. You're doing well. So come on now, cheer up, and let's figure out how to beat the Modern team once and for all!'

We made some changes to our game strategy and switched some of the positions around. Suchi was brought in to replace Sheela. She'd actually mellowed quite a bit. She was still aggressive, which sometimes helped, but she'd stopped pushing and yelling, thanks to Abha Miss.

I looked towards the crowd and grinned to see that almost everyone was holding a muffin or a puff. Way to go, Empire Stores! The teams weren't allowed to eat, though I could see that the Modern School coach had bought a box for them to eat later. I'd already told Mamma to keep aside some muffins, puffs and cream rolls for our team.

The whistle blew and we went back onto the court. And this time, we did slay them. It happened a few times at practice when we were really enjoying ourselves—we worked together like a well-oiled machine. We passed perfectly, we shot like pros and we could see that the Modern girls were hopping with frustration.

We won the game 22-14.

But my joy was shortlived. I should have got my first clue of something being wrong when I looked around and saw that the crowds had dwindled. But I was too exhilarated to think about it. I suppose even if I had, I'd just have thought people had got bored and gone away.

It was Ayesha who said, 'What's going on?'

I followed her gaze and saw Indu Miss and Palak Nanda in animated conversation with my mother. What was Mamma doing here? Foolishly, the first thought that came to my mind was that the bank had sold off our house.

Then the Modern School captain, Veena Bisht, came over and said, 'Well done! Lucky for us we didn't eat during half-time. Was that your plan? To poison us so we would lose?'

'You lost anyway,' said Ayesha. 'And we have no idea what you're talking about.'

'Are you deaf or what? I just told you. The snacks were poisoned. Do you see those kids there? Puking? It was after they ate those muffins.'

'But those are our school kids, so—' Ayesha started saying, but I didn't wait to hear the rest.

I was getting lightheaded with panic. I ran towards my mother. Behind me, I could hear Ayesha yell out my name.

When I got closer, I saw that my mother was in tears. 'I don't know how to apologise. I can't imagine what could have happened.'

'It's very *very* unfortunate, but I'm sure you'll get to the bottom of it, Ms Chinoy. We'll get the girls checked by a doctor, of course, but it does seem like there was something wrong with the muffins.'

'Yes,' said Indu Miss. 'It was definitely food poisoning. Are you sure you didn't use any ingredients that were past their expiry date?'

'I'm sure, I'm sure! But I'll check again. I can't tell you how sorry I am.'

'So are *we,* Ms Chinoy. We understand how important this is for you, and of course we will support you, but you must see that we have a *responsibility* towards our girls.'

'Does that mean ...?'

'We're really sorry, Ms Chinoy,' said Indu Miss, 'but until you can give us a report on how this happened and assure us that it will not happen again, we cannot allow you to supply the canteen.'

The evening meeting, which ought to have been a celebration of victory, looked more like a wake. Oroon, Vir and Nadeem had come to the store, and we were all sitting on the steps outside. Maitreyi and Elizabeth looked rather wan. They had eaten a muffin each and Elizabeth had puked violently. Maitreyi had just got nauseous, and now had a headache.

Everyone was being very commiserative and saying how sorry they were that this had happened.

'We should really try and figure out what happened, though,' said Ayesha.

'Are there any lizards in the bakery? I once heard about a lizard that got caught in one of those manual sugarcane machines in Pune. People fell really sick,' said Maitreyi.

'Maybe a rat got in?' asked Vir.

'No way,' I said tersely.

I was beginning to get a bit annoyed. We have one of those old-fashioned clay ovens, built into the wall. But it's in pristine condition. We always tease my father about having OCD, the way he goes on about cleanliness and hygiene in the bakery.

'Let's go into the bakery and check it out in any case,' said Ayesha. 'Maybe we'll find some clues.'

I knew they were saying these things with a genuine desire to help, but the more they said, the madder I got. And the madder I got, the less I wanted to be around people.

'Look,' I said, as calmly as I could, 'I know you're trying to help, but I can bet anything in the world, that whatever it was could not have been caused by rats or lizards or lack of hygiene or past-expiry-date ingredients. And now I really—'

I was just about to get up and go away, when Nadeem asked, 'But there had to be something in the muffins, right? The kids began to puke after they ate them. That's established, innit?'

That's when it hit me. The clue would lie in the muffin. I went in and got the box my mom had kept aside for the team. She had brought it back with her.

We broke the mufffins open, and sniffed at them. They smelt rather nice.

'How did you feel when you ate them?' Oroon asked Maitreyi and Elizabeth.

We listed their symptoms:
- metallic taste in the mouth
- nausea
- vomiting
- headache
- dizziness

'These sound like the symptoms of carbon monoxide poisoning,' said Nadeem.

'Or food poisoning,' said Oroon, wryly.

'But maybe it was some specific poison,' said Elizabeth, thoughtfully. I fetched my father's laptop, and we spent an hour looking through the net. By the end of it, our heads were spinning. There were so many possibilities, we were none the wiser. But when the boys left, they took a couple of the muffins with them.

'There's this boy in our class who's a complete chemistry nerd. He might be able to check out the muffin and tell us what's in it,' Oroon said.

When everyone had gone, I went in and found my father in the bakery, examining it from top to bottom.

'This place is as clean as it can be. I don't understand.' He sounded so tired and defeated.

My father kept aside the rest of the muffins, to get them officially tested at an FSSAI-approved lab later in the week. He explained to me that there was an organisation called the Food Security and Safety Association of India that ran or supported food-testing labs all over the country. He had a friend in the Lailapaani lab, so he was going to ask him to test the muffins.

On Sunday evening, when the girls came, my mother came to our table with a batch of heavenly-smelling muffins.

'Who's prepared to be a guinea pig?' she asked.

My mother had conducted an experiment: she had used exactly the same ingredients, and followed the same steps and made a smaller batch of muffins. Now we had to try them and see if they made us sick.

They didn't. They were delicious and wholesome and the boys came just in time to get the last of them. Lucky for them that Vir didn't come, so Nadeem and Oroon got one each.

We'd kept aside one for the lab, so that it could be compared with the contaminated one.

'And now for our news!' declared Oroon, licking the last crumbs of the muffin off his fingers. 'So John G says that there's some kind of agricultural pesticide in it. He couldn't separate—'

'Isolate,' interrupted Nadeem, spraying bits of muffin as he spoke.

'Eww, Nadeem, just keep quiet till you finish,' said Elizabeth.

'Yes Nadeem, don't be gross. Yeah okay, so "isolate the compound" were his words, but he's sure it's some kind of phosphate-based pesticide, in a diluted form.'

'There's no way a pesticide could have got into our

muffins,' I said. 'This is definitely sabotage.'

The boys had to leave early, but Ayesha, Maitreyi and Elizabeth stayed on and we tried to figure out what could actually have happened.

The diluted pesticide could have been injected into or poured onto the muffins. To do that with one hundred and fifty muffins would take a lot of time! The easier thing would be to put it in the batter, but my mother had been in the bakery through the whole process.

'But couldn't someone have done it when she turned away for a minute?' was Elizabeth's question, and I had to admit that was possible.

We had two helpers in the bakery, a father and son, and they were vaguely related to some old friend of my father's. They'd been with us forever. What were they going to gain by helping to shut down their source of livelihood? Unless they were given lots and lots of money! But I couldn't even begin to imagine that Firozbaba or Sambhai would do something like that. Not to us.

'They're the only ones who had the opportunity,' said Ayesha.

'And money is powerful persuasion,' said Maitreyi.

'But wait! Firozbaba wasn't there that day!' I remembered. Which was why Mamma was stuck in the bakery throughout.

'That somehow sounds even more suspicious,' Elizabeth said.

'How? How's that more suspicious? It means he had no

opportunity.'

'Maybe the son wanted to do the sabotage thing and he knew the father wouldn't let him, so he gave him something to make him fall sick so that he had to stay at home.'

'Rubbish!' I said. But Elizabeth had put the thought-worm in my head and it wouldn't go away.

So after the girls had left, I walked down the hill to Firozbaba and Sambhai's house, carrying some soup, which I coaxed out of Mamma, as an excuse.

Sambhai was not there, which was good, because if he was guilty he wouldn't appreciate my snooping.

'Aiy, dikra, why did you bother? You should have just told Sam, he'd have come and fetched it,' said Firozbaba, pinching my cheek with his knobbly fingers, like he always did. I wouldn't take it from anyone else, but he'd been doing it since I was knee-high and I barely noticed it now.

'I wanted to see you. How are you? You didn't come to the bakery yesterday and today?' I asked. I told my conscience to shut up. I did want to see him, though I probably wouldn't have come if I hadn't wanted to squeeze information out of him.

'I'm okay. Just my arthritis acting up. I woke up with bad joint pains, couldn't get out of bed.' Not pesticide then, I thought with relief. 'I wish I'd been there yesterday, though. I heard what happened. Sam told me. He was very upset!'

'He was? I mean, of course he was. It was terrible.'

'What will happen now? Will we lose the school order, dikri?' And to my horror, a tear rolled down his cheek. 'I know, I know things are hanging by a thread. What will happen to Empire Stores? What will happen to Sam and me?' It was a positive deluge now and I felt like running away.

Fortunately, Sam came in, looking like thunder. He froze when he saw the scene. 'You been upsetting him, Mahrukh?' Well, yeah, not so fortunate.

'N-no, w-why would I?' I stammered, sidling towards the door. 'Bye, I was just leaving. Bye, Firozbaba.'

I ran all the way home, but I couldn't forget what I had seen sticking out of Sambhai's pocket. It was a brochure about pesticides.

8

At school the next day, people were still in the mood to celebrate our victory over the Modern team.

'Way to go, Mahrukh!' Girls from senior and junior classes, whom I didn't even know, high-fived me as I passed.

Everyone seemed to have forgotten the disaster with the muffins. In fact, I heard a lot of wailing and whining in the canteen because there were no muffins!

'You know what happened on Saturday, no?' Canteen Aunty screamed at them. 'So soon you forgot? You, Chetana, how much you were vomiting! Forgot?'

I wanted to shrink into an atom. Ayesha slapped me on the back. Hard. What's with that girl and violence?

'It's okay, chill,' she said.

Chetana was talking loudly to anyone who would listen. 'I once had such severe food poisoning after eating at McDonald's that my mum still doesn't take me there. But that doesn't mean I'll stop eating burgers there, no? I used to go every day from my old school and stuff myself, without telling her. We had a McDonald's right next to school. And I never fell sick again.'

Another girl said, 'Exactly. Just because it happened once, we'll never eat Empire muffins or what?'

'We should go to the school admin and tell them we want the muffins back,' Chetana said.

Someone started chanting 'We want muffins! We want muffins!' and it soon became a roar.

I dragged Ayesha and Maitreyi out with me. Elizabeth had gone to the library.

'If we're seen there, people will assume we started it. Or at least that I started it.'

We went to the library and found Elizabeth deep in conversation with Miss Zaveri. That girl is very strange. Before we all started hanging out together, she was always cooped up in the library with Miss Z. Now she's a bit more normal.

'Come and listen to this!' she called us over. 'Miss Z was near the canteen when your van came on Saturday and she says that the delivery boy said something very odd. He was late, so Canteen Aunty asked him why. He said they had a puncture at Picnic Point.'

We looked blankly at her.

'Picnic Point?' she said pointedly.

I finally got it. The other two, being non-Lailapaanians, didn't, and were still gaping in bafflement.

'Picnic Point is in the opposite direction from Empire Stores,' I explained. 'To come to school from Empire, they don't need to go anywhere close to Picnic Point.'

'So what were they doing there?' Ayesha and Maitreyi chorused.

'Right?' asked Elizabeth. 'I was just telling Miss Z about our discovery of the pesticide in the muffins, and she remembered this.'

She told Miss Z! No boundaries, I tell you. But I guess I shouldn't complain. This was a clue. And Miss Z was such a recluse herself that there was no fear she would go blabbing to anyone else.

By the time we left the library, the Muffin March had reached Palak Nanda's office. We skirted it and went back to class the roundabout way. I didn't want to be seen anywhere near them.

We had English after the break and Tanveen Miss was in a state of what I can only describe as ecstasy. 'Guess who's coming to visit our school next week!' she said and she was so breathless with excitement that I thought she might need a nebulizer.

'Shahrukh Khan,' yelled one of the class jokers.

'NonoFawadKhan,' Rakshita piped up. 'He'sbetterlooking andabetteractor.'

'But he's Pakistani,' some idiot said.

'So he'll come from Pakistan,' someone else retorted.

Poor Tanveen Miss had lost the class, as she frequently did.

'Miss, give us a clue, Miss,' said Ayesha.

'Let's play twenty questions, Miss!' said Maitreyi. 'Is it a female?'

Miss picked up a ruler and smacked it on the table repeatedly till everyone shut up.

'I can't tell you how upset it makes me that I have to use this ruler in Class VIII. Now, are you going to listen?'

'Yes, Miss!' we sang.

'So this week, we're going to have a special visitor in school!' she said, and before the guessing games could start again, she announced, 'Aruna George, the famous writer, environmentalist and activist!'

Elizabeth was beaming, so she clearly knew who it was, and Maitreyi squealed. 'OMG, I've read her book, it's awesome!'

Some of the girls were nodding their heads. I'd heard of her, of course, but I hadn't read her book. I knew of her mostly because Shernaz was a big fan and had held forth once about something she'd written about big dams and ecology. I remember thinking I should read her some day.

The rest of the class looked unmoved. 'She's staying with us for a whole day,' said Tanveen Miss with undiminished enthusiasm. 'We must make the most of it!'

At home that evening, Mamma gave me the good news: 'We can supply the school again. But we have to make sure there are no repeats of the Saturday disaster.'

We were starting the following week, because we wanted to get all fresh ingredients. No chances.

On the day of Ms George's visit, we had a special assembly. Some senior girls talked about how big dams in the mountains around Lailapaani had changed the monsoon patterns in the region. Elizabeth and Maitreyi had put together a presentation on the dwindling forests. The two of them had spent hours in the library, gone to meet Ms Sultania and talked to Elizabeth's father. It was a very good presentation, but very depressing!

The forests were disappearing fast. The animals had mostly migrated to the other side of the mountain, where there was a Reserve. The tree cover was getting thinner and thinner. Many species of trees and plants and insects were disappearing!

The main causes were tourism, encroachment and illegal tree-felling. In the parts of the forest where tourists were allowed, there was so much plastic and garbage thrown into the valley and along the mountain slopes that entire ecologies were being disturbed.

I was looking miserably at the pictures in their presentation, when something caught my eye. Elizabeth was talking of an encroachment that had been foiled by the Forest Department. They had got the court to stop construction. But the site still remained fenced, because the case wasn't over. In the few seconds that the slide was on the screen, I thought I saw something that looked familiar. I almost yelled 'Stop!' but even Palak Nanda would not have stood for that, so I kept quiet and fidgeted in my seat for the rest of the assembly.

I didn't get a chance to cross-check what I'd seen until the next day. We were in the computer lab, and I asked to see the presentation again.

When they reached the slide with the foiled encroachment, I asked them to stop.

'What is it?' Maitreyi asked.

‘There was something,’ I muttered, feeling a little stupid, because I really hadn’t been able to figure out what it was. I just remember getting that déjà vu feeling, when you know you’ve seen something before, even if you can’t recall where or when.

I peered at the screen. There was a half-built structure, which the builders had had to abandon when the litigation began. There was some kind of signboard that said something but a part of it was obstructed by a car. It was a very fancy car. And that’s when it hit me.

It was a Mercedes. It was the car that I had seen Mr Sisodia get into when he left Empire Stores the other day! I had no idea what it meant or if it even mattered, but it seemed eerie to me that I was suddenly seeing Sisodia everywhere.

After school, I went with Elizabeth to her house. Maitreyi and Ayesha sulked a bit because they couldn’t come, but I couldn’t bear to wait till they were free.

‘You’d better give us a very detailed report,’ Maitreyi said as they waved us off at the gate.

We spent an hour chatting with Elizabeth’s father. He gets kind of excited when any of us turns up. I think it’s because Elizabeth has always been such a loner. She only had one friend, right upto Class VII. So he thinks he has to keep us happy in case we ditch her because her father isn’t giving us enough nimbu paani.

But he was really helpful. We got a lot of information on Sisodia. He was a big-time real-estate tycoon and builder, with a lot of political connections, so he managed to get permissions to build a mall and a commercial complex on what was actually forest land.

The Forest Department filed a case and they had to stop.

'But I think he's in huge debt and his promoters are putting pressure on him to complete the project. So I heard he bought the land from Brigadier Gomes. Unfortunately for him, it's not big enough for the proposed project. Which might be why he's desperate to get the land on which Empire Stores stands.'

'And he must be pressed for time?' I asked, trying to make sense of it all.

'Definitely. He must be running against the clock. He could not only lose the project, but the promoters could sue him and demand their money back. And it's not a small amount. It must run into crores.'

Now it all fell into place! That's why he couldn't wait for the auction. That's why he needed to make sure we got desperate enough to sell. I was sure that it was Sisodia who was behind the pesticide in the muffins.

But how was he doing it? And how could we prove it?

9

We had a meeting at our usual spot near the basketball court the next day and told Ayesha and Maitreyi all that we'd found out.

'See, I was right about him,' said Maitreyi.

'How?' Elizabeth asked. 'You said he was a poacher.'

'Poacher, encroacher. Same thing.'

'I don't see how it's—'

'Girls, girls!' Ayesha raised her hands. 'Let's focus. So we know that this Sisodia guy is desperate to get Empire Stores into trouble, so that they'll be desperate to sell and then he can swoop in and take the land.'

I think I might have gone a bit pale at the thought. I certainly felt a little lightheaded. Maitreyi gave Ayesha what we call her Indu-Miss look.

'What? We have to face facts. Sorry, Mahrukh,' Ayesha muttered.

'No, you're right. It's pretty certain that he's behind the basketball match day fiasco. But how do we prove it?'

'More importantly, we have to prevent it happening again,' said Elizabeth. 'There's someone giving Sisodia information about the orders. So he's going to know that the canteen is ordering muffins again. Have you figured out if it's the bakery helpers?'

I shook my head. I hadn't told them about the pamphlet I'd seen in Sambhai's pocket. Despite everything, I couldn't believe that he could be conspiring against us.

We made some plans for Monday, which was when the muffin deliveries were starting up again. Ayesha and Maitreyi were going to take permission to stay with me on Sunday, and Elizabeth would join us in the morning.

At basketball, there was a bit of a storm brewing.

The tournament was coming up at the end of the term, and we were all on edge about it, ever since we learned that we were playing mixed teams. It was one thing to win against the Modern girls. But if their team was a mix of girls and boys, how were we going to beat them?

Suchi had started talking to the other girls and many of them were now convinced that we would have to play a more aggressive game to win against mixed teams. And we would have to play all-boys teams too. Like Baldwin.

The next day was Saturday, and Abha Miss had arranged a friendly match with the Baldwin boys. We were discussing strategy and plays, when things came to a head.

'There's no point talking about all this. It's just talk. We have to go there and fight!' said Suchi. Many of the others nodded.

Abha Miss looked at them calmly. I was hoping she would

say something to shut Suchi up, but she didn't. 'So what are you suggesting, Suchi?' she asked instead.

Suchi ranted on about how all this careful planning was too technical and would never work against a team like Baldwin. I saw Abha Miss watch the others as Suchi spoke, and I knew she was upset at the way people were nodding and agreeing.

'Right. So Suchi, for the game tomorrow, I'd like you to be captain. Let's try it your way. Tarini can be vice-captain. Mahrukh, Ayesha and Tarini, I expect you to listen to Suchi and follow her lead for this match with Baldwin. Are you okay with that?'

We nodded. I don't know about the others, but I trusted Abha Miss completely, and if she wanted Suchi to lead and us to follow, I was sure there was a reason for it.

When we entered Baldwin the next day, I was thinking about what Oroon and the others had told us about the coach. I was slightly apprehensive. But when we got there we were told that the coach hadn't come. The captain of the senior team had been put in charge in his absence. His name was Pranay Menon. He was over six feet tall, with gangly arms and legs and a head that seemed very small for his body. It made him look like a strange kind of insect.

'So you like him? You like him?' Ayesha poked me with her sharp elbow.

'Why? What is wrong with you? Why would I like him?'

'Because he looks like an insect?' she giggled. I snorted with laughter. I did have a bit of a thing for insects. I liked picking them up and watching them walk around on my hand.

'A little difficult to pick him up,' I said, giggling at the thought.

He swaggered over to where we stood, but when he started talking to Abha Miss I could see his attitude change. He was clearly in awe of her. I grinned at Ayesha, who waved her hand in front of her face, like a fan. I felt total empathy with the Insect, though. The more we worked with Abha Miss, the more I admired her. She was calm, determined and she worked as hard as any of us. She wasn't strict and she never lost her cool, but she still managed to keep all of us in line.

I wasn't sure about this idea of making Suchi the captain, though. Half the girls were pleased, because Suchi had convinced them that her aggressiveness would work better than our planning. The other half, who had bad memories of Suchi's rough game in the old days, were very apprehensive. We all knew how vicious she could be, if she was not controlled.

Ah well, the boys could take care of themselves.

We did our warm-ups and I was just getting ready to go on to the court when Suchi dropped her first bombshell. She wanted me on the bench. I looked at Abha Miss. She shrugged, expressionlessly.

Ayesha and a couple of others began to protest, but Abha Miss interrupted. 'She's the captain, it's upto her.'

I nodded and sat down with the other reserves. Strangely, it didn't bother me as much as it should have. I was curious to see how this game played out. I told myself it might even turn out to be useful to sit on the sidelines and watch the Baldwin boys. If we were going to play them in the tournament, I might get insights into their game that I couldn't if I were in the thick of things.

Abha Miss sat on the bench with us. Insect was the referee, which was okay, since it was not a serious match.

As it turned out it was more than serious—it was deadly. Suchi was back to her old, violent form and the boys were not going to let her get away with it. Soon everyone was playing a rough game, with a couple of exceptions. The fouls piled up and by half-time, many of the players on both sides were limping.

Abha Miss's fists were clenched throughout, but her face remained impassive.

At half-time, when the girls limped up to the bench, she got up and said, 'Let's go.'

Our mouths fell open.

'But Miss!' wailed Suchi. 'We can easily catch up. We're only a few points down.'

'We're not leaving because we're losing. We're leaving because all of you,' and she swept an arm to indicate the boys as well, 'have made a complete mockery of the game.'

She strode over to Insect and said something, and the boys turned to watch us leave. I heard some of them snigger and someone yelled out 'Losers!' When I turned to see who it was, I saw Insect cuff one of the boys on the ear. Right. Way to discourage rough play.

We walked in silence all the way to school.

We thought we'd get a lecture once we reached school, but Abha Miss just told us to disperse. 'We'll talk on Monday,' she said ominously, and walked away.

On Sunday evening, Ayesha and Maitreyi came over for our pajama party. Elizabeth couldn't come, but Oroon and Vir turned up for a bit.

We didn't talk about the match. Not at all. It was in the air, but I think everyone was a bit embarrassed at how they'd got carried away. I knew from watching objectively that Oroon had really been trying to keep his cool, but Vir had given in completely and Ayesha had lost it at least once. Nadeem had got quite a bad head butt from some girl—I hadn't noticed it, so didn't know who—and was feeling a bit out of it. I suspect it was his ego that was wounded, and not his stomach or chest or whatever.

Instead, we talked about our discoveries and suspicions about the muffins. We told the boys how we were going to patrol the bakery in the morning, to get to the bottom of it.

'But what will you do if you catch the culprit red-handed?'

We looked at each other. We hadn't thought beyond the catching.

'The first and most important thing is to make sure that the muffins that get to school are not messed with,' I said. I couldn't begin to imagine what would happen if girls got sick again after eating our muffins.

The next morning, we were up really early. We went into the bakery. Sambhai and Firozbaba were there, of course. I kept a keen eye on Sambhai. We tasted the batter, we tasted the muffins as they came out and generally made a nuisance of ourselves.

But at least we were convinced that this lot of muffins was clean. No pesticide, no nothing.

We waited for Elizabeth, because she had said she would join us in the morning, but she didn't turn up, so we set off for school.

When we reached school we couldn't see her anywhere. Assembly was about to begin and Indu Miss was very strict about people being in time. In Class VII, Elizabeth had overslept and turned up late one day and Indu Miss had made her write an essay as punishment. I don't know if she ever did write it, but Indu Miss spent most of the term saying, 'Elizabeth, essay!' in her terrifying way whenever she saw her. So no, Elizabeth would never be late, if she could help it.

By the time assembly was over, she still hadn't turned up.

'This is most unlike her,' said Maitreyi, worriedly. 'We have the presentation of our Showcase and you know how she is about assignments.'

'She must be sick. Must have overeaten at that Mallu birthday party she went to last night,' said Ayesha as we made our way towards the classroom.

We were walking through the grounds, when a bush hissed.

I stopped. 'Did you hear that?' I asked.

'Pssst!' said the bush again.

I went around, and found Elizabeth. Ayesha and Maitreyi had walked off. I was about to call them, but Elizabeth dragged me behind the bush with her.

'Let them go. No time!' She was panting. I suddenly noticed that she was dishevelled and her cardigan and uniform were covered in muck. She smelt weird too.

'What ...?'

'Don't ask,' she said tersely.

'Don't ask what? Oh my god, what happened to you?'

Ayesha had come back to see what was going on.

'A lot. A lot,' said Elizabeth.

Ayesha took a deep breath and looked as if she regretted it. 'Okay, here's what we do. We have the class presentation in two minutes and people will notice if we're missing. So Mahrukh, go to class, and you and Maitreyi have to make sure our absence goes unnoticed. You—' she pointed at Elizabeth, 'come with me to the hostel and get cleaned up. I can't hold my breath for much longer.'

I ran off, fingers crossed. I quickly told Maitreyi what was going on.

'Oh good god, but how? How are we going to deflect attention from Ayesha? She's the one who has to show the website to Miss and explain what we've been doing!'

As if on cue, Miss Eileen asked, 'Where's Ayesha?'

'Er ... Miss, she had to go to the computer lab, Miss.' I said the first thing that came to my head. 'She needed to get some pictures on ... on the pen drive, Miss, she said she'd come as soon as possible.'

'And Elizabeth has gone with her,' said Maitreyi quickly.

'Okay, so why don't you all tell me what each of you has contributed to the project, while we wait for them,' said Miss, and we sighed in relief. This would give the two of them a good twenty minutes.

But they were back in ten, Elizabeth looking weird in

Ayesha's uniform, which came upto her midcalves.

Ayesha did her presentation and soon we were all engrossed in discussing the project and planning what needed to be done to various sections of the presentation. Luckily, Miss Eileen was very pleased with what we had done.

I was desperate to know what was up, but we had basketball practice soon after.

'We'll see you at break,' Ayesha said, as we rushed off.

In all the excitement of the morning, we had forgotten the Saturday fiasco. By sheer luck, I was in the clear, thanks to the benching. But Ayesha was a bit nervous.

'It's okay,' I told her. 'You only pushed that bully because he was trying to elbow you. You didn't start it.'

'Yeah, but I should have kept my cool. You would have,' she said, looking at me.

'We'll never know, will we?' I grinned. I wondered if I'd have kept my cool if I'd been playing. I would probably have walked off the court in protest. That wouldn't have gone down well with Abha Miss, either!

Abha Miss was waiting for us. Boy, did we get it. I thought I'd escaped because I was on the bench, but clearly that little detail wasn't going to save me from the tongue-lashing. She made us all feel like measly little worms with no minds of our own and no sense of right or wrong.

'Violence,' she said, 'is the resort of cowards.' She said some very harsh things, and she said it so calmly that it made it much worse. The most scathing thing she said though, was about how we'd failed as a team. 'I could see that you were divided. As a team you need to stay together, no matter what. Just because you don't like your captain's decisions, you cannot let your team down. If you don't have one another's back, you're not a team, you're just a loose bunch of losers.'

To our surprise, she didn't single Suchi out at all. I was a bit worried that Abha Miss would kick her out for the way she'd led the team. I'm not a great fan of Suchi's, but she is actually a really good player. Once she reins in her aggression, she tends to be fierce and focused, and we needed her. So I was glad.

At the end of the lecture, we felt drained and in no mood to play anything. But Abha Miss made us do some trust drills. I don't know how she knows exactly what to do. When we started the drills, we were all feeling a bit surly and out of sorts with one another, but at the end, that team feeling was back. She's really amazing.

Before she let us go, she said, 'I want you all to promise me one thing. That no matter what the provocation, you will never resort to violent and unruly behaviour on court.'

'Promise, Miss!' we all yelled, and I noticed that Suchi yelled louder than all of us.

We spent half the break looking for Maitreyi and Elizabeth. Finally, we went back to the basketball court, and sure enough, there they were, sprawled on the bench, hogging muffins.

'At least we know they're okay,' I said. 'We eyed them like hawks this morning, so there's no way they could have any chemicals or anything in them.'

'That's where you're wrong,' said Elizabeth. 'The

adulteration or contamination or whatever, never happened at the bakery.'

And finally, Elizabeth told us about her morning adventure.

Elizabeth was a little late getting out of the house.

'Dad was in his gourmet mood,' she said, glumly.

Elizabeth's dad went to work after she and her mum left for their respective schools—her mum worked in the Baldwin administrative office. So he always made breakfast, and sometimes he'd get into the mood to make fancy things like waffles or Swiss rolls. Elizabeth always reached school panting and panicked on those days.

Anyway, so she had to drop the idea of coming to Empire, because she figured we would have left. Instead, she took the route around the hill, which was slightly shorter. As she was turning into the road that goes past Picnic Point, she saw two men waiting there.

'Guess what they were carrying!' she asked.

'Just tell us,' I said. I was in no mood for guessing games and was impatient to know where all this was leading.

'They were carrying a can of the type that Ram Kishore Bhaiyya uses. You know, that stuff he sprays on the plants?'

'Pesticide!'

'Exactly. I didn't know what to do. They didn't know me, so they kind of ignored me. I decided to go a little ahead, where the lane curves, and hide behind a bush to see what was going on.'

'Seems to be your day for hiding behind bushes,' said Maitreyi.

I shushed her.

'I'd just turned round the curve, when suddenly a lot of things happened. I saw the Empire Stores van coming into the lane from the other side. And alongside the van, there was a man on a scooter. It's a very narrow lane. I had to jump off it, otherwise I'd have been run over. The man on the scooter saw me and recognised me, I think, because he shouted something at me. But that's when I jumped, so I fell into the bush and there was a lot of muck there, maybe even some cowdung ...'

'Definitely some cowdung,' said Ayesha.

'Anyway, so the man yelled, I jumped and maybe because they realised I'd seen them, the men standing in the lane began to run off. The scooter chap yelled again, and the van suddenly stopped, and reversed off all the way to the main road and headed towards the school. The scooter turned around and went with it. I waited for a few minutes to make sure the coast was clear, then came to school.'

I was getting a very uncomfortable feeling in my stomach. 'Did you recognise the man on the scooter?' I asked.

'Nope, he was wearing a balaclava.'

'What colour was the scooter?'

'It was an old Vespa. Orange and white.'

Just as I had begun to suspect. I guess my face showed my misery.

'What is it, Mahrukh?' asked Maitreyi. 'Do you know who it was?'

I nodded. 'Sambhai,' I said. 'He rides a white and orange Vespa.'

I don't know how I got through school that day. I didn't know what I was going to do with this information. Should I tell my parents? Should I talk to Firozbaba? Should I confront Sambhai? My head was whirling.

Elizabeth had to pick up her stuff from Ayesha's room, so I waited for her.

'I can't believe Sambhai could be working for Sisodia,' said Elizabeth.

'But what other explanation could there be? Sisodia must have offered him a lot of money.' I told her about the brochure I'd seen in his pocket. I hadn't told anyone because I was hoping it would turn out to be nothing.

'So what are you going to do?'

That was the million-dollar question. Ayesha and Maitreyi thought I should confront Sambhai head on. But Elizabeth felt it would be best if I told my parents and let them deal with it.

To get to Empire Stores, I had to pass Firozbaba and Sambhai's house. Sambhai's scooter was not there. 'I'm going to talk to Firozbaba,' I decided.

'Do you want me to come?' Elizabeth asked.

I thought for a moment, then shook my head. 'No, you go home. I got this. I'll tell you about it tomorrow.'

Firozbaba was making hot cocoa and insisted I drink some. 'Something is bothering you,' he said. 'Here, drink this and tell me about it.'

We drank our cocoa in silence. Well, almost silence. Firozbhai slurped his down through his missing teeth, and it made quite a racket. I smiled into my mug.

Finally, he put down his mug, and asked, 'How is your friend, that Elizabeth? I hope she didn't hurt herself when she fell?'

I started so badly that I nearly dropped my mug.

'H-how do you know about that?' I asked.

He looked confused. 'No, no, I don't know. Did she fall? I just heard ... I don't know anything.' He began to get very agitated.

'It's okay, it's okay, it's okay, Firozbaba,' I said. I took his mug and went into the kitchen to wash both the mugs. And there, on the kitchen counter was the brochure I'd seen in Sambhai's pocket.

I felt dizzy with confusion. Was Firozbaba involved as well? He had to be! Otherwise, how would he have known about Elizabeth?

He was muttering in the drawing room, as I went in. 'Gadhedo, gadhedo,' he was saying and beating his forehead with his palm. I went and held his hand.

'Don't do that, you'll hurt yourself. And who are you calling a donkey? Me?' I asked, trying to make him smile. But he looked up at me with stricken eyes.

'Don't tell Sam I told you. Promise you won't.'

I was so confused. I promised and left, no wiser at the end of the visit than I was at the start.

I went and sat on the parapet outside the shop. I didn't know what to think. Could Sambhai really be the one who was sabotaging our school contract? Is that why he didn't want Firozbaba to say anything to me about Elizabeth?

Pappa came out and asked if I wanted to go to Mall Road with him. I got into our rickety old Fiat and we set off for the market. A lot people grinned and pointed as we passed, but I was used to that. The Fiat looked ancient and quaint in the midst of all the fancy sleek cars around us. But Pappa kept it in fine condition.

When we reached Mall Road, Pappa went down the dank steps that led to the traders' bazaar. I waited at the car. I didn't like the traders' bazaar much. It was cramped and dirty. And I loved watching the people on Mall Road. There were several contingents of boys from Baldwin. They must have been on some collective outing—they were usually only allowed out on weekends. And the younger ones had to go out with chaperones even then.

I was looking to see if I recognised anyone from the basketball team, when I saw something that made my blood freeze. It was Sambhai and he was with a couple of very slimy looking characters. I ducked behind the car so he wouldn't see me and then pulled out Pappa's phone, which he'd left with me, and took a few photographs.

They seemed to be having some kind of argument. As I watched it got more and more heated, and the next thing I knew, Sambhai was pushed by one of the slimes. He fell down quite hard. Forgetting about my plans to stay hidden I ran towards him. By the time I got there, the two men had left. Sambhai had sat up, but he looked a bit stunned.

'Are you okay? Are you okay, Sambhai?' I asked.

'I'm okay. What are you doing here?'

'I came with Pappa–' I began.

'Where? Is he here? Did he see?'

I explained to him that Pappa had gone into the bazaar. He looked relieved.

'Has this got to do with the pesticide?' I asked. I don't know where that came from. I hadn't intended to say anything.

'What do you know about that?'

But before I could reply, Pappa came up. 'Arre, Sam, you're also here? Come back with us.'

He declined, because he'd come on his scooter, and we parted ways. But he looked at me as he left and I knew this wasn't the end of it. Thinking about it on the car ride back, I thought he looked more puzzled than guilty.

In the morning, when the baking began, I went to the bakery again. Sambhai snatched a moment when no one else was around to ask me what I knew about the pesticide. I said wasn't going to tell him until he told me what he was doing at Picnic Point yesterday.

He looked at me for a moment, as if trying to decide something. 'Okay,' he said. 'I've told your father that the delivery boy is sick and I'm going to do the canteen delivery today. You can come with me in the van.'

We didn't have time for any more talk. I didn't know what to make of this.

I got ready quickly and went with him.

'Is your friend okay?' was his first question.

'Yes, no thanks to you,' I shot back.

'I didn't know whether to go back to her or follow the van. But I needed to make sure the food reached the canteen safely, you must see that. Otherwise, many girls would have fallen sick again. And I'd seen those rascals running away, so I knew she was in no danger from them.'

'But I don't understand what you were doing there! Why were you there?' I asked.

'See, I knew that there was something very fishy about what happened on the day of the basketball match. You remember that new delivery boy, Ramesh? He suddenly called and said that he couldn't come and his cousin would come instead. I didn't like the chap on sight, but that was nothing, so I kept quiet. When that whole thing with the girls falling sick happened, I got suspicious. So I kept an eye on him and I heard him laughing and saying something to someone on his phone about a pesticide. So I went to the Krishi Udyog shop and got a brochure.'

'Oh, so that's why—!' I blurted.

'Yes, I thought you must have seen it in the kitchen yesterday.'

'N-no, yes,' I said, embarrassed. I didn't tell him I'd seen it much earlier and had been suspecting him ever since!

'Anyway, I realised that pesticides could cause vomiting and sickness. And the only way anything like that could get into the muffins was if it was done along the way to the school. So I followed the van. But when we turned into the lane, I saw your friend there. I panicked a bit. I thought they might hurt her, because she was a witness ... I didn't really think clearly. I accelerated and started shouting. The rascals ran away and Elizabeth fell, and in that moment I decided to follow the van. At least, the boy got frightened and went straight to school, so it kind of worked out okay.'

'What if you'd caught them red-handed? They would have hurt you, then! What were you thinking, Sambhai?'

'It was all just suspicion at that point. So I couldn't tell anyone and I wasn't sure what was going to happen ... but you're right. I should have thought it through.'

'And yesterday evening?' I prompted.

'I thought I'd seen one of those men in Aminbhai's hardware store once, so I went looking for them there. I asked them who had put them up to doing this, but they wouldn't tell. I don't think they will do it again, though. They're scared.'

'We should go to the police!'

'I don't think so. I didn't even tell your father, because with all the stress about the house, I don't want to worry him more. I'm quite sure it won't happen again.'

We reached school then, and I got off.

'Thank you, Sambhai,' I said. And I meant for more than the ride.

Before we knew it the mid-term break was upon us. We always have the mid-term break around holi.

Ayesha left for Delhi, very excited, less about seeing her folks and more about being able to download more hip-hop music and meet her old friends who shared her love of rap. We were all quite bewildered, and in Elizabeth's case, downright disgusted, by hip-hop and rap, and it really bothered Ayesha.

'You people need to get with the hip-hop scene. I can't believe I'm friends with such a bunch of nerds.'

She'd told us about this all-women hip-hop group from the 80s called Salt-N-Pepa which sounded cool. And someone called Tupac, who is supposed to be very famous, but whom I'd never heard of before.

'What? You haven't heard of Tupac Shakur?' She started rapping—the lyrics sounded angry and rebellious. But also poetic. I could see why she liked it. It was very Ayesha.

It was fun listening to her, but we just couldn't get as excited about hip-hop as she was.

‘At least my friends in Delhi get it,’ she said sulkily.

But she was a bit jealous that the three of us would be in Lailapaani together through the spring break.

‘You’re going to play holi without me!’ she wailed, as we waved her off.

I never play holi, but this time Maitreyi took over the planning. No one had a choice once Maitreyi started channelling her inner Indu Miss. And there was a lot of it to channel, thanks to genetics.

So the plan was that we’d all gather at Empire Stores. Oroon and Nadeem would join us there. Vir had gone home for the break. Mamma was going to pack us a hamper, and we would all head to Elizabeth’s colony, where holi celebrations were taken very seriously. There was an assigned area, and even a tank of coloured water to dunk people in. It all sounded very stressful. I wasn’t looking forward to it.

But Maitreyi wasn’t listening to any arguments about how bad for the environment it was and how yucky it was to have people pat your face down with colour when you didn’t even know their names.

‘Stop being such a snob,’ she giggled. I didn’t think it was funny.

So on the morning of holi, there we were, Elizabeth and Maitreyi and I, at Empire Stores, waiting for the boys. We waited and waited. No sign of them at all.

‘Why don’t you call?’ Elizabeth asked Maitreyi.

She called from the landline in the store. They put her through to the boys’ hostel but someone came on the line and said Oroon was not in the hostel. Neither was Nadeem.

Maitreyi looked worried. 'They seem to have left a while ago. Should we walk towards Baldwin and see if we can find them?'

We stuffed some macaroons in our mouths to sustain us on the journey and began to walk leisurely up the hill towards Baldwin. It was a beautiful day. It wasn't cold any more and the flowers were in full bloom. All the gardens were bursting with reds and purples and oranges. But what I liked best were the clusters of little yellow and white flowers that grew wild on the hillside. They reminded me of childhood walks with Shernaz, winding up and down the hills, through forests and fields, many of which were now built up.

The town looked quite unattractive now, with the higgledy-piggledy construction, badly painted houses, the profusion of cheap hotels and garbage everywhere. But then in the middle of all that, the yellow and white flowers bloomed, simple as something painted by a child, and reminded me of how much this town was a part of my life.

I was so lost in this mawkish line of thought that I didn't notice the gang until they were upon us. They were a boisterous lot—I knew a couple of them by sight, because they were regulars at the shop, but the rest of them were strangers.

'Holi hai!' they shouted, like it was some primitive war cry and suddenly we were surrounded. Elizabeth started whimpering, Maitreyi screamed, though I couldn't make out if she was screaming with laughter or fear or both. I did what I do best. I ran. Up the hill, I went. But before I got very far, I heard footsteps pounding behind me. Two people—one girl and one boy—caught me by the hands, while another girl poured a bucket of coloured water over my head. I closed my eyes and let them.

But if they thought I was going to let them get away with it, they were mistaken. While they were pouring the water, I put my hand into my pocket and found the packet of gulaal I had kept there. A little soggy now, but so much the better! When the girl had emptied the bucket and the other two let go of me, feeling very pleased with themselves, I launched myself at them.

They looked like three red-faced baboons by the time I was through with them. They took it well, though. They yelled 'Happy holi!', high-fived me and ran off downhill to join the rest of their gang.

I ran down too, to see how Elizabeth and Maitreyi had fared. Both of them were lying on the ground and I speeded up, my heart thudding. Were they hurt? These holi gangs can be quite unpredictable. What had I done? Had I abandoned my friends? Again? They never let me forget the time I'd left them in the forest, disgusted with their bickering. Would they completely disown me now?

When I got closer, I could hear Maitreyi gasping. Elizabeth was muttering, 'Shut up, shut up, shut up.' Then Maitreyi looked up and to my relief, I realised that she was laughing.

When she got her breath back, she told me she had collapsed on the ground in hysterics, because Elizabeth had got colour on her glasses and had spent the entire time squeaking, 'I'm blind! I'm blind!' as she tottered around with her arms outspread.

'But I *am* blind!' Elizabeth wailed, refusing to get up off the ground. 'I can't see anything.' She wouldn't budge till

I'd run down to Empire and got a bottle of water to wash her specs with.

Maitreyi had sobered down and was back to wondering what had held Oroon up.

'They must have got waylaid by holi gangs, just like we did,' I said and suggested we stick to our plan. 'We can leave a message for them to join us at Elizabeth's later.'

We collected the hamper with the goodies, our change of clothes and the colours and pichkaris from Empire and headed off to join the holi celebrations in Elizabeth's colony. We dropped off the hamper at Elizabeth's first. A bunch of people were already in the tank and we jumped in too, thickening and colouring the water, which already looked less like water and more like liquid grease. Rakshita was there too, and I recognised my tormentors from earlier. They waved cheerily and we waved back.

We splashed around, got dunked and squirted on, did some dunking and squirting back. At the end of it, all of us looked like strange alien creatures, with the whites of our eyes and our grinning teeth standing out in stark contrast to our dark, colour-streaked faces.

Back at Elizabeth's, we washed and changed and sat down to eat, still looking a little pink. Elizabeth's father brought us hot chocolate to drink.

'Where's Amma?' asked Elizabeth.

'Some trouble at the school; she had to go,' said her father.

'At Baldwin?' asked Maitreyi. 'What happened?'

'The usual, I suppose—some boys up to some mischief. When they have to talk to parents and all that, they always call Mary. She knows many of the parents, so it's easier.'

Maitreyi caught my eye and I knew she was thinking what I was thinking: was this why Oroon and Nadeem had not showed up? Had they got into some kind of trouble?

Elizabeth's mother came back a little later, looking really tired.

She told us that a boy had had to be taken to hospital because he'd been injured. His parents had to be called and she had had to wait till they drove up from Behrampur.

'Did you see my brother there?' asked Maitreyi.

'He's in the basketball team, no?' she asked, looking at Maitreyi with an odd look in her eye. 'The boys in the basketball team are talking to the principal. Nobody knows what happened to Chintan, the boy who got hurt. We think it happened in the basketball court, but the boys are saying they didn't see anything. It's all a bit puzzling.'

'They were supposed to come here and play holi with us,' Elizabeth told her mother.

'I don't think that's going to happen,' Mary Aunty said.

So we went to Elizabeth's room, munched on chips, sipped on lemonade and speculated about what could have happened, until we fell asleep, exhausted from all the playing, shouting and eating.

When Maitreyi and I met Oroon and Nadeem the next day at the bakery, they looked ragged at the edges. Elizabeth had family stuff going on and hadn't been able to come.

They wouldn't tell us what had happened to Chintan, at first.

'It was some bad shit,' Nadeem said, 'but we've promised not to talk about it to anyone outside the school.'

‘I bet this is something to do with your coach,’ Maitreyi said.

Oroon and Nadeem looked at each other. They seemed uncomfortable.

‘Okay, don’t say anything,’ I said. ‘Just nod if we’re right.’

Nadeem put his head down and stared at his shoes, but when we looked at Oroon, he gave a quick nod.

After much coaxing and cajoling, we got some information out of Oroon and Nadeem.

The coach had lost his cool over some trivial thing and hit Chintan across the face. The boy had a severe gash across his cheek and forehead. The coach had gone home immediately after it happened, and told them to tell the principal he was sick.

‘I hope you aren’t going to sniffle and snitch like little girls. Remember you have to come back to the basketball court tomorrow,’ he’d said, as he was leaving. I actually saw red spots before my eyes when I heard that!

The principal called the entire basketball team and grilled them for hours, but they all said they’d seen nothing.

‘We don’t know, Sir. He must have fallen down,’ they said. Every one of them just repeated the same words. The principal knew they were protecting someone, but he couldn’t do a thing.

The principal thought that one of the other boys had beaten Chintan, but since the boys refused to talk, he couldn’t figure out who it was. He checked all their knuckles, apparently!

We were aghast.

'Why didn't you say something?' asked Maitreyi.

They had no rational answer. Apparently, it was against some stupid Baldwin School code. It was against all reason and sense.

I can understand not complaining about your schoolmates—that's just nasty.

But when a teacher bullies kids, it makes my blood boil. It's like people being cruel to dogs and cats. They can only do it because the poor, dumb creatures can't hit back. But no matter how much Maitreyi and I argued and urged the boys to complain, they refused.

'Okay, then do what you like. It's your funeral,' I said, furious.

Before they left, they made us swear we wouldn't tell anyone else about it.

'Not even Elizabeth and Ayesha,' warned Oroon. 'Elizabeth's mother might get it out of her. And Ayesha will be up in arms and there's no knowing what she'll do. And Maitreyi, definitely not Mum, okay? You know what will happen if she gets a whiff of this.'

So we kept the horrible secret to ourselves, much against our will.

12

The days after the spring break passed in a blur.

Apart from the usual classes and projects for each subject, we were also fine-tuning our presentation in class for the end-of-year Showcase. On the basketball court, the excitement was building up for the tournament, which was to take place in the last week of the term.

All the schools in Lailapaani were coming, and two schools were driving up from the plains. We were nervous and excited, but with Abha Miss pushing and pulling us, we put all that nervous energy into our game.

'You know,' I said to Monica, Tarini and Ayesha one day, after we'd had a particularly good practice session, 'there's something almost poetic about the game, when it's going well.'

They screamed with laughter, which was not quite the reaction I was expecting.

'Okay, okay, there's no need to get so hysterical. You guys are useless. I bet Abha Miss would get it.'

'What would I get?' Abha Miss said, from behind me.

Gah.

The girls cracked up again.

'N-nothing, Miss,' I said. My ears felt like burning coals.

'Miss,' Ayesha hiccupped, 'she ... she says basketball is like p-p-poetry!' And they all fell about again like she'd cracked a really funny joke.

Abha Miss smiled indulgently. 'Don't mind them. They're comedians. It's true of anything, you know, from mathematics to carpentry to wrestling. When it's done elegantly, there's a kind of rightness to it. You could call it poetry.' And she left.

I raised my eyebrows superciliously at the girls, but that only set them off more. So I gave up and giggled along with them. I could kind of see why what I said was funny, but I could also kind of see that it was true.

We didn't meet Oroon and gang at all. Maitreyi and her mum went out with Oroon one weekend. Maitreyi said that their coach had been working them really hard for the tournament. They had completely stopped coming to Empire. Things were working out well at the store, at last. The school orders seemed to have really upped our demand all over town, and orders were pouring in. The interest had been paid, and there seemed a good chance that we would stay afloat.

Sometimes I remembered Sisodia and wondered if he was up to something. He wouldn't give up so easily, surely? But I shrugged off the thought. There was too much going on.

And then, when there were four days left for the tournament, I fell sick.

I couldn't believe my luck. I caught a bad cold and cough and had a slight fever. So no school, no practice, nothing. Abha Miss sent me a message through Elizabeth: 'You have three days to get well.'

'Sounds like a threat,' said Elizabeth.

But I held on to the thought. By the third day, my fever was gone and my cold had dried up. My voice was still hoarse. But I didn't need a voice to play basketball. So on the fourth day, despite my parents' mild protests, I got up, got ready and went to school.

'Will you be able to play?' Abha Miss asked me. I wanted to say yes. But I knew I was a bit weak.

'I don't know, Miss,' I whispered. Not because I was emotional or anything, only because my voice was gone. She nodded, as if I'd given her exactly the answer she'd expected.

There were six schools coming. Baldwin, Modern and Hill School, of course, and three others. There would be three mixed teams, two all-boys' teams (Baldwin and AVB) and one all-girls' team (us).

The teams were divided into two groups, A and B, of three teams each. Each team in a group would play against every other team in the group. Then the winner of A would play the runner-up of B, and vice versa. The two winners would then play each other.

The team captains were called to pick up chits, which would allot their team to Group A or B.

We got Group A.

We watched anxiously to see who else would be in our group. Baldwin was B. The Lailapaani Govt School was B.

Modern was next. Their captain was a boy. He picked up a chit.

'Let it be B, let it be B, let it be B,' I prayed. So of course it was A.

Vishwabharati was the other school in our group. Which meant that AVB Boys was in B. Good, I thought. Let the boys battle it out.

The tournament would go on for five days. On the first three days, there would be one Group A match and one Group B match each. So at the end of three days, all the three teams in each group would have played against one another.

On the fourth day, there would be two matches, where the winners of A and B would play the runners-up of B and A. These would be knockout rounds. So the losers would be knocked out of the tournament.

On the fifth day would be the finals.

I really really hoped we would make the finals.

'But don't think about that now,' I told myself. One match at a time. Except, I wasn't going to play the first match.

There was another picking of lots, to see who would play whom first. The three chits would be numbered 1 to 6, Group A would get numbers 1 to 3 and Group B would get 4 to 6. And the order was to be:

Day 1: 1 plays 2, 4 plays 5
Day 2: 1 plays 3, 4 plays 6
Day 3: 2 plays 3, 5 plays 6

Modern picked first, and they were 2. So they would be playing the first match. Then LGS picked and they were 6.

So the two boys' teams would definitely play first. Baldwin got 4. It was Tarini's turn next. She picked a chit. I forgot to breathe.

She opened it and sighed, 'Three.'

Ayesha did her elbow thing, but I was too busy breathing to care. We didn't have to play today! Which meant that if I was feeling better, I might even be able to play our first match.

Before we began, Palak Nanda came to the centre of the court. All the teams and the spectators were sitting around the court. She had a hand-held mic. I hoped she wouldn't speak for long. I was impatient for the matches to begin.

'I'm so *thrilled,*' said Palak Nanda, 'to be hosting this tournament in our school. I hope you will all enjoy playing in these *lovely* surroundings, with the trees swaying and the birds chirping. Because that's the beauty of sport. It helps you *appreciate* the outdoors. Before we begin, I have an announcement to make. I know that sports are usually win-lose affairs and bring out the *competitive* instinct in people, but we at Hill School would like to do this differently. Why can't sports be about *playing*? Why can't it be about enjoying the physical *and* the mental dimension? Why can't it be about participation and *fair* play and sports*manship*? So we have decided that the scores alone will not decide who goes into the next stage of the league. In addition to the scores, the winners will be decided on the basis of other qualities as well.'

There was a chorus of 'WHAT?'s around the court. We all looked at one another with expressions that must have been comical to an outside observer. The Hill School girls were probably less shocked than the people from the other schools. We were used to these strange pronouncements from Palak Nanda. I looked at the teachers and coaches from the other schools, wondering if they had been warned. Clearly not. They had their mouths open. I had to stifle a giggle.

I looked at Abha Miss, and caught her looking at us. She had a quizzical smile on her face. I wasn't sure what to make of it. I concluded that she was probably told just this morning, and she was kind of amused. But who knows, maybe it was her idea all along. Meanwhile, Palak Nanda, oblivious to the shock and horror around her, went on.

'We will have two observers who will judge the teams on parameters like sportsperson-like behaviour, equitable participation, elegance and grace.'

Huh? Elegance? Grace? Was this going to be like one of those ice-skating competitions? Would we have music?

'By grace, I don't just mean physical grace. I mean *graciousness*. Let's not be aggressive in sports. For too long sports have been fields of *battle,* spawning almost warlike violence. Let's make sports a thing of *beauty*.' She smiled beatifically at the stunned crowds, and announced:

'And now, I declare this basketball tournament open!'

The thunderous applause was missing. Some people clapped half-heartedly. Most of the teams had gone into desperate huddles to try and decode the Palaknandese.

'Is she serious?' asked Ayesha, shaking her head in disbelief. 'This is out of the park, even for Palak Nanda!'

Suchi was fuming. 'What's the point of all that training and practice? If scoring baskets is not going to make us win, then why bother? How is this basketball?'

I didn't care really. For me, basketball had never been about winning. It was all about the game.

'Look at it this way, guys,' I croaked. 'Now we can actually enjoy the game, without worrying about the score.'

The whole team turned and glared at me. I threw up my hands and shut up.

It was clear right from the start that there were essentially two tournaments going on. There was the one that existed in Palak Nanda's head, where teams were judged on beauty and grace and whatnot. And there was the one being fought on the court exactly like the battle she spoke about.

The Modern versus Vishwabharati match was first. Both the teams were pretty good. There were two girls in the Modern team–including Veena, the captain of the girls' team, who was an outstanding player. But she barely got to touch the ball. The boys only passed to each other, and ignored the girls completely.

Veena was not our favourite person after the way she talked to us at the end of our earlier skirmish, but we all felt indignant on her behalf. Somewhere in the middle of the first half, we began to shout, 'Pass to Veena! Pass to Veena!' Veena looked startled at first, but when we carried on, she shot us a smile. And suddenly I felt a great affection for Palak Nanda.

Modern won on points, but the match was not over. The two judges were Ahmed Sir and Eileen Miss. They came onto the court and analysed the game.

'Modern has scored more than Viswabharati on the scoreboard. But the Modern boys were not passing to the girls at all. We're deducting points for that. Viswabharati also loses points for aggressive play. There was some shouting that was uncalled for ...'

In the end, Modern won by a sliver.

The next match was Baldwin versus AVB. It was an all-boys affair, so there were no points to be lost for passing, we thought.

Wrong. AVB were still pulled up for not passing fairly to everyone. They had one weak player, who was clearly there as a filler, so they never passed to him. That lost them points. A bit of a damned if you do, damned if you don't situation for them.

But what set that match apart was not the game, but the Baldwin coach. All the girls had become starry-eyed on seeing him. 'He looks like a prince,' Monica breathed in a nausea-inducing way.

But once the game began, he turned into a toad. He screamed at his team, and at one memorable moment, even cuffed one of them on the ear as he passed by. The boys looked terrified, but the screaming egged them on and they played a pretty rough game. It was painful to watch.

Baldwin won on the scoreboard, but they lost by two points. It didn't make a difference at this juncture. But when it came to making it to the knockout rounds, Palak Nanda's insane rules were going to matter. They'd have to win their next match and AVB would have to lose *their* next match, and even then it might come down to the scores.

The next three days passed in a blur. We scored so many baskets against Viswabharati, that though we lost a few points for shouting (yes, shouting, I kid you not!), we still won.

On the third day, we had to play against Modern School. To our surprise, they fielded three girls and two boys, instead of the other way round. Their reasoning was transparent, and stupid. They should have been playing their best players, irrespective of gender. Not more girls for a match with a girls' team. That's just foolish. We were not a weaker team because we were girls, and if they couldn't see that, they were being blind.

The match was really close, though. I think we got a bit over-confident after our easy win against Viswabharati. We gave away a lot of lollipop shots and we missed some really good chances. But we fought back, and by the time there were ten minutes left, we were ahead by four points. Which is not a great lead. We had to hold on to it, and keep the pressure up, if we were to win.

Modern School had taken off one of the girls and brought in one of the boys, and he had clearly been told to play an attacking game. He was taller than all of us, which made it a bit difficult to stop him, but Abha Miss had taught us a few tricks.

We managed to keep him from scoring right until the last two minutes. Then Tarini made a huge blunder. She misjudged a throw and it went to one of the Modern girls, who passed it to the tall boy. And basket.

A lead of two, and two minutes to go. We were all very tense. Everyone watching the game had gone quiet. Two minutes is a very long time in a basketball game.

With one minute to go, Ayesha passed the ball to me. I turned to move towards the D, but I was blocked. I couldn't turn again. I looked around for someone to pass to but there was no one. Veena was right in front of me. I feinted to her left, as if I was going to pass to Suchi. She fell for it. When she half-turned, I jumped up and took a shot. It was a long, long shot. The ball arced through the air, and went straight into the basket. Airball!

'Up yours, Modern!' Ayesha screamed, as the whistle blew.

After a moment of shock, we all started laughing. Which only made it worse. We lost.

Five points were deducted for that yell and five points for laughing. But like I said, there were two matches going on. We felt we'd won one of them.

Even Abha Miss seemed more amused than angry when she told Ayesha to try and control her tongue. Ayesha was quite abashed.

'Sorry, guys. I was just so excited that I lost it,' she moaned.

Luckily, as it turned out, it didn't matter. Modern School topped our group, but we came second. In Group B, Baldwin lost to AVB, but they made it to second place too. So Baldwin, AVB, Modern and Hill School would play the knockouts. Modern would play Baldwin and we would play AVB in the first round.

Modern lost to Baldwin and AVB lost to us. Which meant the finals would be played between Baldwin and Hill School.

As we lined up on the court, I spotted Oroon, Vir and Nadeem in the Baldwin line-up and raised an eyebrow. Oroon raised one back. Nadeem raised both and Vir scowled. They all looked nervous.

Before the match, Palak Nanda gave another little speech about sportsmanship and graciousness and all that.

'Please remember, we are not here just to *win*. We are

here to play as *friends*, not as adversaries. The *playing* is as important as the outcome of the game. So let us be friendly and play a *happy* game.'

I think it was aimed at the Baldwin coach. Everyone was appalled at Hiro's aggressiveness. He stood on the sidelines and shrieked—there's no other word for it—at his team. I don't know if it helped. They just seemed to get more harried and make more mistakes. In the last match, which Baldwin played against Modern, he had yanked one of the boys off the court by his hair.

The game began, and so did the yelling. It was horrible. We couldn't focus and I think it was worse for Ayesha and me because we had friends in the Baldwin team. They flinched every time Hiro yelled at them, and it made us very uncomfortable. Because it was the finals, he seemed to have become even more frenzied.

At half-time, when we huddled around Abha Miss, Ayesha said, 'Miss, this is impossible. How can we play with that man screeching and hopping?'

'That's how most matches are in the real world,' said Abha Miss. 'So deal with it.'

I looked across at the Baldwin boys. Something was going on there. The boys had all gathered around and something was happening in the middle. We could see Hiro, because he was taller than the others, and Insect was there too. Hiro was shouting at someone.

Suddenly, all the boys yelled. The crowd parted and we saw Insect carrying a boy. He seemed to be unconscious. He put him down carefully on the ground and shouted, 'Someone get an ambulance!'

Indu Miss and Abha Miss ran to where the boy lay, Indu Miss shouting at one of the kids to fetch the school nurse. Ahmed Sir was on the phone, calling an ambulance.

Hiro swaggered over to where the boy was lying and sneered, 'Such delicate mama's boys. Can't take a bit of rough handling.'

The other boys in the team were all standing around.

'A *bit* of rough handling, Sir?' asked Insect, and he sounded really angry.

'What exactly happened?' asked Indu Miss.

The boys all started talking together. We were trying to listen but Abha Miss came and told us to move away.

So we stood and watched while Indu Miss spoke, first to the team, then to Insect and finally, to the coach. Hiro seemed to be getting agitated. Ahmed Sir joined Indu Miss and Abha Miss as they talked to Hiro. Then he took Hiro towards the school buildings—to the staffroom, we assumed. We were desperately curious to know what was going on, but no one would tell us.

An ambulance came and Prem, the boy who was hurt, was taken away. Our school nurse and one of the teachers went along.

We waited and waited. Abha Miss was talking to Insect and the Baldwin team. Finally, she came towards us. Insect and the Baldwin captain, Manek, came with her.

'There has been ... er ... some issue with the coach, Hiranandani. So he has been ... er ... persuaded to go back. One of the boys in the team has been badly hurt. We thought we should cancel the rest of the match, but the

Baldwin team would like to continue. Manek? Would you like to add something?'

'Yes Ma'am,' said Manek. 'Though a lot of bad things have happened, and Prem, our teammate, has been hurt, we thought we should continue playing. But the Baldwin team have decided that we don't care about winning any more. We want to play this match and just enjoy it. If you girls are okay with that.'

The rest of the match was pure fun. We had such a good time! We were playing to *play,* as Palak Nanda would have said. I wish all matches could be like that.

Baldwin won and we all high-fived one another. It was a game played in the true Hill School spirit.

Palak Nanda must have been a proud principal that day.

We got to know later that Hiro had hit Prem so hard across his ear that he had fainted. He was going to be all right, but his parents were going to file a case against Hiro.

The whole basketball team was going to give testimony, because as the term progressed, Hiro had become more and more aggressive, screaming, hitting the boys, throwing the basketball at them really hard and giving them inhumane punishments when he got frustrated.

He'd once made a boy stand out in the sun for three hours without any water because he'd been late for practice. It was only because his friends figured out a clever plan that he survived. They knew Hiro was keeping an eye on him from the staffroom. But he could only see the boy's back from where he was. So they would send someone to distract him at regular intervals and four other boys, of the same height and build, took turns standing there.

The boys didn't complain because that was the way things were at Baldwin. You were expected to take everything the school threw at you—including abusive teachers, apparently—without complaint or question. Also they were quite afraid of Hiro and if the school authorities didn't listen to them, things would only get worse for them.

Chintan, the boy he had hit during the spring break, had never come back. His parents had moved him to another school. That had made some of the boys wonder if they were doing the right thing by letting the coach get away with it.

In a way, Palak Nanda was responsible for how things turned out.

The boys began to get defiant and questioned his methods during the tournament. At half-time during our match, Prem had said that he felt Hiro should stop screaming, because this tournament was not just about winning on the court. That had set Hiro off.

Some time later, Shernaz found out from her old gang that Hiro was having severe anger management problems when he was at the university in Canada. He had turned violent with one of his classmates and that's why he had been sent back. Because he'd been such a star student, Baldwin had decided to help him out.

They must have been regretting it badly now, because the school was in the local newspapers for all the wrong reasons.

The good news, though, was that he'd been sacked. People who needed their heads examined ought not to be given power over a bunch of kids. Psychology 101.

13

The last day of the term was the day of the Showcase.

There were a lot of very odd 'showcases', because, really, what did it even mean?

So one class did a demo yoga session. 'Because yoga is a holistic exercise of mind and body,' they claimed.

Another class made a terrarium, saying it showed their understanding of biology and also their concern for ecology and the environment.

Another class had practised water dance in the swimming pool. But they had forgotten to tell the swimming pool attendant and he had drained the pool to clean it. So they had to do their dance on a stage. They looked really funny dancing in slow motion, as if they were underwater, in their swimming costumes. Everyone tried very hard not to laugh, because they looked so stricken and earnest.

And so it went on. Ours was uneventful and a bit boring to be honest. Or maybe we just had spent too much time on it.

Ayesha's parents couldn't make it to the Showcase, and were coming the next day, so we were all going to spend the night and all of next day at Elizabeth's house. Her father had promised to take us into the Reserve in the Forest Department vehicle. Oroon, Nadeem and Vir were coming in the morning, and they would join us on the trip.

As usual, Elizabeth's father got very excited and kept coming into her room with food and drink for us.

'Did you hear the news about Sisodia?' he asked me at one point.

I hadn't heard anything.

'He's left the country. There were so many cases against him. Even the Forst Department had some cases pending against him for encroachment and the like. But I think finally he left to get away from the creditors.'

Good riddance.

It had been a really stressful term in many ways, but in many ways it had been fantastic.

Abha Miss had left, but she promised to come back after a year, and stay on for the whole year, instead of just for a term.

'I hope you'll all continue to practise and work hard,' she said at the farewell party the team gave her. 'Some of you have great potential, and I want to see you make it to the national team some day.'

Some of the girls were very excited at the thought of competing in the nationals. As for me, I was happy to just play basketball, hang out with my friends and go home to Empire Stores.

Annual Review

The Hill School for Holistic Learning

Name: Mahrukh Chinoy

Class: VIII

English

Mahrukh is a diligent student, although she sometimes shows a disregard for some aspects of literature. She tends to be frivolous at times, which distracts the other students and also dilutes her own interest in the subject. But if she applies herself, she can excel.

—Tanveen Kaur

Science

Mahrukh has a natural aptitude for the sciences, but her interest lies in the life sciences. She therefore focuses on biology at the expense of physics and chemistry. With a little more perseverance she could be an exemplary science student.

Mahrukh shows a keen interest in the environment and is passionate about the ecology of the hills. She is very knowledgeable about the flora and fauna of the school and its surroundings and this will stand her in good stead if she decides on a career in the environmental sciences.

—Eileen D'Souza and Meenakshi Iyer

Mathematics

Mahrukh is very good at mathematics, but she needs to work harder to achieve her potential. Her ability is not matched by her application, at present.

—*Shabnam Tyrewala*

Social Studies

Mahrukh is competent at geography, but does not show an interest in history, unless it is directly relevant to her. It is important for her to realise that history helps us understand our lives and times with greater depth and empathy. She is not wanting in potential, but she needs to focus her energies on academics. Less basketball, more books.

—*Indu Dasgupta*

Student's Self-appraisal

I worked really hard and achieved my best performance in basketball. I started the term with some difficult stuff at home, but with the help of my family and friends we overcame all the problems. It was a pretty awesome term, in the end.

A. Coven is a hybrid creature. Filmmaker, author, editor and philosopher, she has been to many schools across the country. Her Pathan-Bihari-Mallu-Bong genes and her pan-Indian upbringing make her multilingual and the perfect citizen of Delhi, except that she doesn't live there any more.